DEFENSELESS

To Shauna,

I dedicated this to your Dad. He knew what it really meant to be a tough guy.

Be brave & crazy!

Love,

Pete

DEFENSELESS

A NOVEL

PETER WILSON

BPS books

Toronto & New York

Published in 2012 by
BPS books
Toronto and New York
www.bpsbooks.com
A division of Bastian Publishing Services Ltd.

ISBN 978-1-927483-12-1

Cataloging-in-Publication data available from Library and archives Canada.

Cover: Gnibel
Text design and typesetting: Casey Hooper Design

Printed by Lightning Source, Tennessee. Lightning Source paper, as used in this book, does not come from endangered old-growth forests or forests of exceptional conservation value. It is acid-free, lignin-free, and meets all ANSI standards for archival-quality paper. The print-on-demand process used to produce this book protects the environment by printing only the number of copies that are purchased.

To

Uncle Brooks

CONTENTS

PART 1
RECOVERY

WAKING UP

1 Anyone who's been knocked unconscious knows that waking up from that space between worlds is a weird feeling. You don't really remember anything; you're just happy to be waking up at all.

When I was younger, I used to lie in bed in the morning drifting in and out of consciousness to the sound of water running as my family had their showers. There's something glorious about opening your eyes and being flooded with light after complete nothingness. That's when you're most aware of your sense of sight. You search for answers with your eyes, the answers that your brain has shut out. It's a bit like waking up in the morning after drinking way too much.

But that's not what happened to me. I was knocked unconscious. I don't remember anything about what happened.

As I regain consciousness, my eyes scan the room for anything familiar, anything to help me sort out why I'm in a hospital room. Immediately, the pain radiates from the top of my head, blotting out my thoughts. I must have been unconscious. I'm in terrible pain.

What happened? I quickly check my teeth and nose. My teeth are still there, and, despite feeling broken, my nose seems straight. Through swollen eyes I see Joey talking to a police officer. She keeps pointing to me. She seems upset. I'm so sore. It's mostly my upper body. I'm covered with bruises like the first day I tried snowboarding. Perhaps I was hit by a car. But no, that's not what happened.

Joey sees that my eyes are open and rushes over. She has been crying.

"What happened?" I ask. I sound a little like Keanu Reeves when he surfaces from the illusory world in *The Matrix*.

She's too rattled to explain. "You got beat up," is all she can say.

It's not the most descriptive of sentences, but it does the trick. I don't remember everything, but images are slipping through my mind like shadows on a wall. The color is off, the lighting is dim, but my head is fine-tuning the reception.

I see a figure stomping on my head, like in that scene in *Goodfellas* when Jimmy and Tommy attack Billy Batts. I realize there is more than one figure kicking me as I lie on the ground.

The real world breaks in to distract me when a doctor and a few nurses enter. The doctor begins dishing out directions to the team of nurses.

If you're in the hospital and have several medical personnel working on you at the same time, that's a strong indicator that something bad has happened or is happening to you.

All of a sudden, I feel sick to my stomach. Whatever is inside my stomach is soon going to be on my stomach. I try to tough it out, but a nurse like an angel summons up a plastic bowl for me as if she carries one around with her for just that purpose. I make good use of it.

"Thank you," I say, trying to smile.

It's a pretty rare occasion when puking on yourself can make a situation better.

Two nurses are working on my ears. Another is working on something just above my left eye. One doctor is working on something on the back of my head. Another is standing next to Joey. I feel that at any moment, this doctor is going to turn to her, and, like a character in *The Princess Bride,* say, "See, there's a big difference between mostly dead, and all dead. Now, mostly dead is slightly alive."

I'm pretty sure I'm getting stitches in two places at once. I guess my family can't be too bad, because all I can think of is that I want to go home.

The team works on me for a long time, but they all seem to finish at the same moment.

The lead doctor speaks, slowly, quietly, and as if I'm not even there.

"Good work, everyone. I think we should keep him till the morning just to make sure he is all right."

Good work, everyone? All right? I am far from all right.

Shortly after this scene from *ER,* I pass out.

* * *

I wake up again and see Joey. It must be early morning because she's sleeping in the chair beside my bed. I try to fall back to sleep but can't. My body is throbbing.

An old man is stirring in the next bed over. We're separated by just a curtain, so I can hear everything. He's uncomfortable. He starts coughing. Joey doesn't budge; it must have been a long night.

For some reason, lying there in a hospital bed with a swollen face and in extreme pain, I feel like testing the theory that you can learn a lot from old people.

I tug the curtain. "Can't sleep . . . ?"

"Haven't slept through the night in a long time," he says.

"Mind if I pull the curtain?"

"Go ahead."

Judging by his reaction, I must look pretty bad.

"Oh, son, what happened?"

What a nice old man.

"I got beat up."

"I'm sorry to hear that. There must have been a few of them."

"I guess so."

"Do you know who they were?"

What am I doing? On second thought, I don't want this attention at all. I want to crawl into a cold dark hole and heal.

"I don't remember much."

"That's awful. Kids are so violent today. Was she there?"

"Yeah. Unfortunately."

Almost on cue, Joey wakes up. "Baby, how are you? Do you need anything?"

"No, I'm OK. Thanks."

"Good morning," the old man says. Joey could give a shit about him.

"Hey, could I get some water?" I ask Joey.

"Of course. Just gimme a second . . ."

"Here, have some of mine," the old man says. He hands a water bottle to Joey who reluctantly passes it to me. I inspect the bottle like a wine connoisseur checking a vintage. KEEP CALM AND CARRY ON is written on it in bold letters. "What brand is this?" I ask.

The old man's laugh turns into a cough. I reconsider drinking his water. "That's no brand," he says. "It's a slogan from World War II."

When's Remembrance Day? I usually watch *Saving Private Ryan* on Remembrance Day. The water bottle obviously isn't from World War II, so I let the old man explain himself.

"I wrote that on there. There's something comforting about it."

"I'm going to get a doctor and see if we can get you home," Joey says.

I like the sound of that. With luck I'll get some painkillers.

After Joey leaves, the old man moves closer. "Listen, when you recover, don't go after the guys who did this to you. Revenge doesn't make anything better."

Revenge? I don't even know what happened yet.

Joey returns with a double play: a doctor and painkillers. She's the best.

The doctor says I'm fit to go home but to come back and get my stitches out in a few days. Joey helps me stand up. I'm still wearing my street clothes. My shirt is ripped and crusted with dry blood.

Even the medical staff can't help but stare at my face as I walk down the hall. In a weird way, I'm looking forward to looking in the mirror.

Joey must have called a cab, because there is one waiting for us at the exit door.

What am I going to tell everyone? Maybe Joey has already done some damage control for me. At the rate I saw her clicking away on her BlackBerry, she must have sent the whole city an APB on what happened to me. I'm the only one who doesn't know. I'm going to find out, though. That's the thing with girls — they're talkers. That's why there are so few females in the Mafia. They'd all turn state's evidence. But I guess even my favorite New York gangster, Mickey Featherstone, turned state's, too. When I was younger, the first time I saw *Goodfellas,* I thought that was a happy ending.

As the cab pulls away, it becomes immediately apparent that this is not going to be one of those silent cab rides.

"What happened?" the cabbie asks.

I go with the answer that seems to be working. "I got beat up."

"You're a big guy. There must have been a few of them."

There must have been, but I don't want to talk about it, especially with you, cabbie. I catch glimpses of my face in the side window, but all I can see is a white bandage around my head covering my ears. I had no idea it was there.

"Well, I hope you find the guys."

Joey is looking out the window. I take her hand. She turns and smiles. She has a lot on her mind. She must be waiting for the right time to tell me what she saw. I just want to take some pain medication, sleep in my own bed for a while, and watch some movies. Then I'll ask her what happened.

"I'm OK," I say. It's a weak attempt at comfort.

She makes a crooked smile as if to say, "No, you are not."

We're getting close to where I live. I wouldn't call it home, because I'm at university and living near campus. For me, home is where my parents and brothers live, about two hours away.

What am I going to tell them? Maybe I don't have to tell them anything. I broke my hand in first year, and I'm pretty sure they have no idea. I don't want them to know about this either.

Once in my apartment, I flop onto my bed. The cold pillow is soothing, and I don't want to be parted from it. But Joey says, "You should put a towel on your pillow in case you bleed while you are sleeping."

It occurs to me that "Bleed While You Are Sleeping" would be a great name for a death metal band.

The towel is not as comfortable as the naked pillow, but I'm glad I'm not going to wake up to a stained pillowcase. I lie down, and Joey joins me. I can't sleep. Maybe the painkillers will help. I take some. I put on the movie *Fear and Loathing in Las Vegas*. It's an odd choice, but there's something comforting about watching someone manage to function on drugs while you're on drugs, too.

Before I put the movie on, I finally check myself out in the mirror. I look like the thing in *The Goonies* except that may be too flattering. I almost consider yelling, "Hey, you guys!" It looks as if someone inflated my face with a bicycle pump. For some reason, I smile. That makes for an interesting contrast.

I can't go out looking like this. Not even a good pair of aviator sunglasses and a baseball hat could hide my injuries. I guess I'll be missing class on Monday. It's a good thing I got a trusty doctor's note. In the academic community, at least at university, a doctor's note and a good story can go a long way. I need to work on my story, though. "I got beat up" has a certain stigma attached to it. People would rather be entertained.

Joey will help me improve my story. I know that behind her eyes is a traumatic experience just waiting to be released. For now, all I have to do is heal. I can do that. I've always been very good at lying around and sleeping.

I'm in so much pain, though. The sooner the painkillers kick in, the better. Right now it feels like the skin on my upper body is burning. I didn't ask for this. I think of Gwen Stefani singing about how all she ever wanted was . . .

A SIMPLE KIND OF LIFE

2

I wake up from a dreamless sleep and feel considerably worse than I did before I dozed off. My memory is returning, and it's no comfort.

I remember walking down the street holding hands with Joey. I remember some idiots yelling from across the street. I remember wondering why they didn't have anything better to do that night. I remember letting go of Joey's hand, and that's it so far.

Joey feels me moving around and wakes up. She is, as usual, lovely.

"Hey, baby, how are you feeling?"

"What happened?"

Joey immediately begins to cry. I hate seeing her, or any girl, for that matter, cry. But her crying is so genuine you want to save the tears.

"It all happened so fast, and it was dark. It's tough to remember."

I'm patient. I know it will come. She collects herself and starts: "These two guys were yelling at us from across the street.

They were being really rude for some reason. I told you to let it go, but you left me on the sidewalk and went over to them. You started arguing with them, and then one of them pushed you. You pushed him back and started like wrestling with them both. But then, out of nowhere, like four more guys came around the corner."

Shit, this is going to be tough to listen to, and she is far from finished. Her sobs act as punctuation. I second-guess myself, wondering if I really want to hear this part of the story.

"The four guys came up behind you and one of them punched you. I guess you got knocked out, because you fell straight back and hit your head pretty hard on the ground."

I guess that explains some of the stitches. But that doesn't explain why I had to have my ears drained.

"Then the six of them start kicking you while you were on the ground. I was yelling at them and screaming for them to stop, but they wouldn't. Other people started noticing what was happening, so they ran off. Then I ran over to you and I was holding your head. Someone must have called the police, because a cop car and an ambulance appeared. They put you in the ambulance and took you to the hospital."

I feel pathetic and embarrassed. I'm in this much pain, and for what? I could have just kept walking. I could have just held on to Joey. Only one word comes to my mind and that is "unnecessary." I'm gradually filling with rage. Joey can see it in my eyes and hugs me. "I'm just glad you're all right," she says.

All right? I am far from all right. I'm going to get those guys. I'm going to find them, and I am going to kill them. But I have to relax. Joey doesn't need any more stress. Just do what every good man in history has done at some point. Apologize to the woman you care about. "I'm sorry," I say.

"Don't be sorry. Nobody deserves what happened to you."

I feel violated. My emotional rage overwhelms my physical pain. I have to fight my urge to go outside and run around the block screaming. I want to ask Joey more questions, but I'm afraid of the answers I might get. She knows I'm upset. In a weird way, this whole incident has shown just how much she cares about me. I feel I don't deserve it.

I get to the point. "Do you remember what they looked like?"

"If I saw them, I'd remember them. Maybe not all of them, but the first two guys for sure."

That's good news. Hold on to those memories, Joey, and forget the other ones. The ones where I am flat on my back, defenseless, and being beaten stupid. The ones where they turned an already unfair fight into a massacre.

"Did you talk to the police?" I ask.

"Yeah, one of them gave me a detective's card. You're supposed to call him."

A minor setback. If movies and books have taught me anything, it is to do your own dirty work and leave the cops out of it.

Wow. Who am I? When did I turn into public enemy number one? For now I need to rest. I have the ace in the hole: time. There's little doubt in my mind that my assailants are enrolled at the university. It won't take long for me to find them in this small community.

"I'll call the cops tomorrow," I say. "Don't feel like you have to stay here with me."

Joey is shocked. She really does care about me. She laughs, even though her eyes look like blue water balloons.

"I have a midterm tomorrow. It may be a little tough to study, but I should go, I guess."

I completely understand. I'm sort of glad she's leaving. I love her company, but after all the attention at the hospital, I want to be alone with my pain medication and Edward Norton movies.

"Call me if you need anything," she says. "I'll come by again tonight to see how you're doing."

She kisses me on the cheek, avoiding my swollen, cut-up lips, and leaves.

* * *

There are a couple of logistical things I want to take care of before I take more pain medication and cloud my head, but a knock on the door interrupts my train of thought. I don't want to answer it looking like this, but there's something compelling about a ringing telephone or a knock at the door.

The older I get, the more I dislike answering the door, and I'm only twenty-one. What a treat of an old man I'll be, answering the door for kids on Halloween. This student-populated area must be the worst place for anyone trying to solicit donations, but there at the door is a woman from some charity I've never heard of. She's startled by my face and forgets her pitch, but soon remembers it.

"Do you think we can stop world hunger?" she asks.

"No, I don't think so."

She starts up again like a struggling gas lawn mower. I cut her off before she can get started. “Listen, I appreciate what you’re doing. I think it’s very honorable. Unfortunately, I don’t have any money to give to your cause. Thanks.”

Perfect delivery. That should send her on to the next house. But for some reason she isn’t moving. I consider pushing her off the stoop. The drugs are taking over.

“I’ve been getting that a lot lately,” she says.

Is she trying to confide in me? I must be so hideously ugly she’s trying to leech some pity. I want to yell at her.

“I hope you feel better,” she says.

I shut the door firmly to let her know how I feel.

I’m not myself, but I have to do this while I look my worst. I go back upstairs and knock on Kevin’s door. Kevin’s my best friend and has been for a long time. Seeing me like this should inspire unspeakable rage in him. He’ll ask me what happened. I’ll make the story better and definitely edit a few details for more sympathy.

Like the charity bitch, he tries but cannot hide his shock. “Hey, how you doing, big daddy?”

Good opener. He already knows what happened but maybe he wants to hear it from me. “I’ve been better.”

Classic. I tell him what happened. I can see his fists clench about halfway through my version. “That kind of thing shouldn’t happen,” he says, sounding a little like Batman.

I agree. I let him know that I’m going to get some rest. To lighten the mood, I make a joke that I recover faster than Wolverine on speed.

I go back to my room. The drugs are really working now, and

I love it. It's times like these you understand why addiction is the human condition. It feels good. But I can't sleep. The drugs should have tucked me right in. My dad always used to say, "Don't feel sorry for yourself," but right now I want to.

I'd love to add to the story that I was minding my own business, but I wasn't. I would have never done anything like this with my own friends. We had done some dumb stuff, even had the occasional scrap with people, but nothing like what I'd been through. I try to think of situations that might warrant that type of behavior, but not many come to mind . . . except for revenge.

I should call my family. I should call my dad. I just want to go home. I'll call tomorrow with a clear head. I need to sleep.

Thinking about not being able to sleep just makes it more difficult to get to sleep. I prayed for *Inception.* What a fantastic skill it would be to fall asleep easily and wake up just as quickly. I had always put that superpower up there with being able to function on a high level when hung over. Everyone knows at least one person who can keep up their normal routine even after a night of drinking. That reminds me that my normal routine is out the window. With that thought, the self-pity returns.

Why me? What did I do to deserve this? Whose karma did I dump on? Where's the bright side to this terrible situation? But that's just it. There is no silver lining. In the movies I'd be given a superpower in compensation for having my body harmed. Then I could return like the Toxic Avenger. As Wooderson said in *Dazed and Confused,* "You just have to keep L-I-V-I-N'."

There's nothing poetic about what happened. Nothing honorable. Just a cloak of embarrassment and some new scar tissue.

I don't want to be myself. I want a DeLorean and Doc Brown. I want to go back in time. But I can't. I just have to lie here, restless and in pain.

I was quick to give Joey the option to leave, but I already miss her. I'll have to take comfort in the paper heroes, along with some scantily clad women, on my walls. I put a poster of Terry Fox on my wall after watching that Steve Nash documentary on TV. Joey thinks the image is sad, but I find it uplifting. Even though my room is dark, I can make out my George Carlin poster. I wonder if Joey knows who he is. I'll have to test her next time she's over.

The self-pity begins to ebb away, thanks to the drugs. All I wanted was a simple kind of life. The self-pity will be back, but meanwhile I drift mercifully into the world of...

DREAMS

3

I'm buried underground. There's no coffin, just dirt all around me. It's in my mouth and nostrils, and I can't breathe. I try to thrash around, but I can't move. I'm suffocating. I struggle, but it's no use.

What was that Alfred Hitchcock TV episode with the guy who escapes from prison in a coffin and is buried only to realize that the person who was supposed to dig him up is actually dead in the coffin beside him?

I give in and accept my death. Then, like being launched from a catapult, I'm above ground, cherishing the fresh air. Having made my *Final Escape,* I fall to my knees taking deep breaths, happy to be spared.

Something hits me on the back of the neck really hard. I fall flat on my stomach, tasting dirt again. I roll over to see an entire baseball team with bats coming to attack me. I don't even like baseball. Maybe that's the problem. It's obvious that one swing was not enough. They're just getting started. I beg them not to hit me again. What did I do?

Their faces blank above their white uniforms, they continue hitting me. Why are they hitting me? I don't deserve this. I hear my bones cracking with each blow and pray for unconsciousness. They pound me until every bone in my body is in pieces. After this, I could be the Blob's stunt double.

Somebody help me. Somebody make the beating stop. I see Joey. Why won't she help me? She's just standing there. Do something! I see her walking closer, and, when she reaches me, the baseball furies walk away. I should be dead. Who could possibly survive this?

Joey doesn't seem the least bit concerned. "Don't worry," she says, "we'll get them next time."

Next time? What next time?

From out of nowhere, she dumps a bucket of water on me, dousing my entire body. The cold water feels amazing. I want it to never end. As the bucket empties, I try to sit up. Much to my surprise, I'm successful. I look down at my legs. They should be covered in bruises and cuts, disfigured by the baseball bats, but they're fine. I check my arms, and they're fine, too. I turn to look at Joey, but she has disappeared.

I stand up, only to be hit with something on the back of my neck that floors me again. I'm on my stomach again, tasting dirt. I can only hope the furies are finished with batting practice.

I roll onto my back expecting the worst, but figure I might as well identify who's attacking me. I look around, covering my head with my hands. A raven lands on my stomach. I flinch but for some reason don't try to knock it off. The raven sits peacefully on my stomach. If Edgar Allan Poe has taught me anything, it's that ravens mean bad luck. Now several other ravens are landing on different parts of my body. Isn't a group of ravens called a murder? Or is that crows? Same thing.

The first raven begins to peck at my stomach. His friends follow his lead. I'm guessing there are as many as fifteen of them. Their beaks are like knives. Please don't peck out my eyes. Nevermore! Joey? Where is Joey to help me?

I see Kevin. He must be coming to help me. As he approaches, the birds fly away. He stands over me and says, "I'm sorry I wasn't there for you earlier, but I'm here now." He reaches back and takes a bucket that has appeared out of nowhere. Yes, the healing water, please.

He pours the bucket of liquid on me, but it smells different — it's gasoline this time. I think of the cop in *Reservoir Dogs.* I scream. Why did he do that? He's my friend.

I hear a match strike and can guess what's going to happen next. I am set on fire and left to burn. I can't wake up. I'm in too deep. I'll just have to ride the roller coaster and hope something will make me wake up.

I am ablaze for what feels like forever. Reminding myself that it's just a dream helps me gain some control. The fire fades out. I look down at my legs. They should be charcoal black. They are, but the black isn't my skin. I'm now wearing a dark suit. Well, I might as well go with it. I need my rest, and if that means sitting through a surreal dream like Maya Deren's *Meshes of the Afternoon,* then so be it. I stand up in my dark suit and tie. Oh, I get it. I'm going to attend my own funeral now. I'll have to tell Joey this one.

Next, I walk to the front of the church and approach the

casket. I've heard that if you die in a dream, you die in real life, but maybe in this case seeing my dead self will jolt me back into the land of the living.

I lean over the casket. It's the old man from the hospital. I didn't see that coming.

I lean over to pay my respects. I wish I knew his name; this may be a dream, but I don't want to be rude. As I'm about to walk away, the old man sits up and yells, "Keep calm and carry on!" It scares the shit out of me. There's no doubt I'm sweating in my sheets. Good thing I put that towel down on my pillow. Towels don't discriminate. Blood or sweat — it's all the same to them.

Having a dead man yell some World War II slogan should have shocked me awake, but it didn't. I'm starting to get fed up. Did Stephen King write this dream?

Still in my dark suit, I'm suddenly running down the middle of a street as fast as I can. I'm being chased by two figures and they're gaining on me. It's too dark for me to get a glimpse of their faces.

The theme of this part of the hallucination is not tough to grasp. I know enough about dreams, even while I'm dreaming, to see that this is the classic chase dream. I haven't had many of them, but I learned from psych class that this is a common theme. The two figures undeniably represent my real-life attackers. Four more guys should join them shortly.

Did you know that the word "nightmare" originates from a female evil spirit thought to suffocate sleepers by lying on them? I guess I was suffocating earlier, and now I'm out of breath from running. But, as Morpheus said, "Do you think that is air you're breathing?"

I've decided to remove myself from this pathetic dream. Do your worst. I'm going to change the setting. Of course I can. It's my dream.

I run past the gates of a long driveway and into a nearby house. I shut the door and lock it. The lights are dim. I can smell cigar smoke. I can't believe it: I'm in Don Corleone's office. I haven't watched *The Godfather* in over a year, but I have all the three-dimensional floor plans of the Godfather's office in brain storage. He calls me over. What's he's going to say to me? Is he going to ask me to whack someone?

"Dreams permit each and every one of us to be quietly and safely insane every night of our lives." A sleep therapist with the last name "Dement" said that. What an appropriate name for someone who studies nightmares. The narrative of this dream certainly supports his theory.

I wish I could download this dream and watch it later, analyze it, and maybe even show it to friends. I'd have to show it to Joey, and Kevin, and maybe even the old man, if he's still alive. I've always thought it would be cool to watch someone else's dream. *Batman Forever* with Jim Carrey as The Riddler and the brain box thing sort of covered that. Maybe I can get to it in the future; for now, I have to focus on the moment.

I turn and see Sonny. I should warn him about the causeway, but the Godfather is about to speak. In that unmistakable voice, he says, "Do you know what is most important in life, my son?"

No, please tell me, wisest of wiseguys. The most important thing in life, he says, is . . .

FAMILY

4 I desperately want to remember my dream. I want to hold on to every detail, every disturbing vignette. But I'm overwhelmed with pain. I forget everything. I can barely open my eyes. They're almost swollen shut. I'm the last person who wants to make a big deal out of this, but I'm badly hurt.

I turn and look at my towel-covered pillow, now spotted with blood. Good call, Joey.

I need painkillers. I go over to my desk where I spilled out my last dosage and take more than I should. I don't deserve this. Nobody deserves this.

Joey enters my room. "How are you, baby?" she says. "I brought you some snacks. Cool Ranch Doritos and cream soda, your favorite combo."

I don't remember having a favorite combo. I try to smile and thank her, but my speech comes out muffled through my swollen lips, and my smile must look like two hot-air balloons colliding.

"How are you feeling?"

"Not great."

"You should call your parents."

I remember part of my dream — my chance meeting with the Godfather and what he said. Maybe I *should* call my family and tell them the story.

My mother is the classic "best Mom in the world." How she puts up with my brothers and me, I'll never know. She deserves a medal. If she heard how her first-born son was beaten unconscious, she might have a heart attack.

My dad's very secretive. Well, maybe secretive is not the right word. Put it this way: He could be Tony Soprano, for all I know. In this case, that might help. He keeps most things private. He likes Western movies, because the cowboys say little and seek justice.

It will certainly upset them both to hear what happened. But why am I special? People are beaten, even killed, every day. Am I being selfish? The world does not revolve around me just because I was assaulted. In a way, I'm responsible. I didn't avoid it. If anything, I walked headfirst into the six-man stomping. Still, I could use some time at home with my family.

"Yeah, do you mind if I call them right now?"

"No, go right ahead."

"You might have to fill in the blanks. The details are still a little bit fuzzy."

"Sure, but do your parents even know me?"

"Of course they do."

I grab my cell phone and make the call. I hope I get voicemail. After a couple of rings, I start thinking about what I'm going to say.

A message queues up in my head: Hey, Mom and Dad, I have terrible news that will most likely ruin your day. I was attacked and beaten to within an inch of my life by six guys. I'm currently lying in bed on painkillers waiting for time to heal all my wounds. When I recover, I'm going to find out who did this and hurt them, bad. I'm going to get help from Kevin and Nick. Remember Nick? He went to juvie for assault at fourteen. I'm going to get them both to help me exact my revenge. I haven't thought up precisely what I'm going to do to them or how, but you always said creativity runs in the family. Call me back. Love you.

What I actually say when I get their voicemail message is, "Hi, Mom and Dad, I have some bad news. I got beat up pretty badly the other night and I'm in pretty rough shape. Please call me; I'd love to talk to you."

"Your parents aren't going to like that message."

"Have you told anyone else about this?"

"Yeah, sort of."

That's Joey-speak for I have told everyone. That's not necessarily a bad thing. The more ears on the street, the better chance someone will tune in if they overhear a conversation about a vicious beating.

"How many people?"

Her eyes start to well up.

Oh no, I broke the dam, and here comes the water. I try to stop it. "Listen, I'll be fine. I just don't want people talking about it. It's pathetic and embarrassing."

She is immediately offended. "Pathetic and embarrassing? Since when is being the victim of a violent crime pathetic and embarrassing? I understand if you don't want me to talk about it, but it helps me deal with it. I had to watch someone I care about get attacked. I had to hold your bloody head in my hands and look at the blank stare in your unconscious eyes."

I'm going to kill the guys who did this. Not because of what happened to me, but for what they put Joey through. She's now in full cry, and that hurts me regardless of painkillers.

She tells me I'm supposed to call the detective. "His card is on your desk."

"I think I'll talk to my family first and see what they think."

I really don't want to speak to the police. I want my six attackers, especially the first two guys, to think that nothing will come of this. I want them to let their guard down. Time is my friend. I can take as much of it as I need to heal and compose myself. Then I will act.

"Do you want to watch some TV?" I ask.

Joey nods, and we go downstairs to the TV room. I hope none of my housemates are down there, but they most likely will be. I grab my cell phone in case my family calls back. Before I manage to struggle halfway down the stairs, it rings.

I make a U-turn for my bedroom and answer the call.

"What happened?" my father says.

It's almost automatic for older people to ask this or "What are you going to do in the future?" no matter what the occasion. Do they really care what you think happened or is going to happen? Do they want the newer generation's take?

I'm a little stunned to be talking to my parents in the state I'm in. My dad has to repeat the question.

I know my mom is listening on the downstairs phone. Any kid who has two good parents knows that there are some things you want to talk to dad about, and there are some things you want to talk to mom about. Unfortunately for my mom, she has three sons. There just aren't many things we want to talk to her about. I swear we got a female dog just so Mom wouldn't feel like a social outcast in her own family.

Hearing Dad's voice makes me want to go home. I guess my lack of response triggered something in his mind. He knows me pretty well. "We're coming to get you," he says, which is followed by the click of the receiver.

What I don't notice until after I put my phone down is that I'm crying. It's the first time I've done that in a really long time. I'd almost forgotten what it felt like to totally let go of my emotions. I start laugh-crying. This definitely doesn't fit the macho angry guy code. I pass the tears off as tears of joy. I'm happy my family is coming to get me.

Sitting in my room with the lights off watching movies while high on Percocet isn't the best way to heal; sleeping in my own bed, having home-cooked meals, is. Going home gives me something to look forward to. That, and retaliation. I'll write that goal down as a reminder for when I return. I pull a blank sheet of paper from my printer and try to think of something poetic. I write, "Don't Stay Noble." Perfect. I tape it to my wall.

I head downstairs, hoping to catch Joey discussing my unfortunate situation with my housemates. But all I hear is the TV. Kevin and Joey are sitting there in silence. Maybe they're riveted by something good on TV. Nope, just commercials. I guess that's what TV has pretty much been reduced to anyway. They must have something on their minds. It must be me.

"Hey," is all I can think of to say when they see me standing there.

Kevin pipes up with, "Hey, how you doing, man?"

"Better. I think my parents are going to come get me."

Joey is thrilled at the announcement.

"A couple days at home, and you'll be back in no time," Kevin says.

I leave and head back up to my room. Joey follows. "You guys seemed to have a lot to talk about down there," I say.

She doesn't even smile. "We're both worried about you. There isn't a whole lot to say."

"Come on, there has to be something to talk about. Some celebrity must have stolen a car or something."

"They could have killed you."

A bit dramatic, but her comment brings a lot of things into focus. Every being clings to life. That's why I can't let this go. That's why nothing else is on my mind. That's why Kevin and Joey are worried about me. Those six guys threatened my survival. My life almost ended. I can deny it all I want, or say it wasn't that bad, but it was.

I look at George Carlin and Terry Fox and smile. "Yeah, but they didn't," I say. "When I'm done with them, they're going to wish they had."

Joey is frightened. "Look, it's only been a few days. But is that what you really want? You want revenge?"

"No, I want to make things right."

* * *

I feel a healing power when my parents knock on the front door. My mom might cry when she sees me, but I've prepared myself for that. I let them in. Like strangers meeting, they first assess everything about my physical appearance. They don't like what they see. My dad grabs my stuff and puts it gently into the car. I smile when I see this. The way he loads the car is a sign that he's enraged.

As I get in the car, I realize that this has been my first time outside in three days. Or is it four? As we pull away from the house, my dad speaks for the first time. "Where did it happen?"

I give him directions. I know only because Joey told me.

Dad pulls the car to the curb at the scene of the crime. I hesitate to get out. I fully expect to see blood on the concrete. The street looks completely ordinary. I have an immediate sensory overload. I see the first two guys' faces clearly. I'll never forget them. I see myself getting beaten. I see myself defenseless.

"Life goes on," my dad says. "It's important to go back to where it happened. Maybe when you're ready, you and Joey can come back here."

Mom is crying but doing a decent job of hiding it.

We all get back into the car to start the drive home. Before we get on the highway, I ask Mom for a piece of paper and a pen. She gives me a napkin and a pencil. That's all I need. I write down every detail I remember about the first two guys. I name them Departed One and Departed Two after the Oscar winner for best picture. Their real names will come later. I have more than enough details to jog my memory and conjure up the portrait I have of them both. An unexpected but great head start to the process of gathering . . .

INFORMATION

5 After only a week at home, I've almost fully recovered. I feel better. I'm off the pain medication and ready to return to school. The week away has been time enough for other gossip and stories to replace mine. It's a humbling fact that, when you're not around, the world keeps on going about its business.

While I was home, I tried to move on. I tried to forget, but it was like a paper cut in my mind. I was happy my younger brothers didn't know too much about it. It would have upset them, and I don't think they would have fully understood because I myself don't fully understand.

As soon as I was off the pain medication, which Dad suggested be sooner rather than later, I got down to consolidating some information. If I'm going to have a shot at getting the retribution I so desire, I have to have a plan.

The first thing I did while I was home was create a training regimen — similar to one that boxers use — to replace some of the muscle I lost in the week and a half of recovery. The university has just spent a ton of money building a new gym. If I just follow this training, I'll be stronger than ever in no time.

This kind of thinking will be familiar to anyone who ever purchased a fitness product from an infomercial at three o'clock in the morning. My motivation is different, though. I'm no Rocky. I won't be drinking raw eggs. But I'm very motivated.

The second thing I did was call up my good friend Nick O'Gallagher. It's tough to know where to start with Nick's life story. Not because the story is complicated but because it's not for the faint of heart.

I went to a big public high school, and anyone who has attended one knows you get all sorts of different kids with different backgrounds. Nick's home life was the standard cliché for a troubled youth. He had a drunken, abusive father and a submissive, fearful mother. He was the younger of two brothers, and his father liked to target him, despite his older brother's attempts to intervene.

Nick was big and strong and as hard as a coffin nail. His philosophy was simple: Don't take shit from anyone. He would pick a fight with three guys and take a beating just to land one punch. That was who he was. I always pictured him rising to the top of the boxing circuit, relying on his ability to take a punch. Don't misunderstand, though. If given an opportunity to strike back, Nick was fierce.

I met him in our homeroom class in high school. Everyone was scared of him, including the teacher. It was obvious that he was not to be disturbed. He might just as well have been wearing a t-shirt that said "Don't Mess With Me." It must have been fate that I crossed paths with Nick and became his friend. The incident served to introduce me to Joey, too.

A group of guys were teasing her. It was nothing serious, but I decided to intervene. I realize that this sounds remarkably like what caused my recent attack. Stubbornness is one of my better qualities. Anyway, I stepped in, and their attention turned to me. I thought I'd defused the situation pretty well, but I guess I didn't, because the same guys were waiting for me outside after school.

Just as things were about to get physical, the guys backed off. Standing behind me was Nick with a smoke in his mouth and a smile on his face. He was about the only one that I remember at school smoking. I turned to thank him. He just walked away. I was an immediate fan. I wanted to know more about him, not because I needed protection but because I could see he was lonely.

To this day, I think Joey said yes to being my girlfriend because I intervened with those guys, so in a way I owe it all to Nick.

The next day, Nick showed up in homeroom with bruises all over his face. I didn't know it at the time, but this was the work of his father. Nick rarely missed a class. School was the only place where his father couldn't get to him. I had to know what happened. I had to show him some compassion, to return the favor.

After class I asked him if he was all right. I was terrified. Every muscle in my body was clenched, expecting him to lash out at me.

"That's none of your business," he said.

"Fair enough. I just wanted to say thanks for what you did for me yesterday."

"Not a problem. Those guys love unfair fights."

"Well, I really do appreciate it and, if you ever need anything..."

He nodded and walked away. We had a few more casual conversations in the week that followed, and everyone started asking me about him. Our friendship was under a spotlight; no one associated with Nick.

A week later, he asked me the question that would cement our friendship and make it possible for me to ask him the big favor. He wondered if he could crash at my place that night.

I was blown away. Nick had completely swallowed his pride. He was sick of his father's physical abuse and wanted a night of peace. He would ask that question more and more often, and my parents never opposed the idea.

I was so shocked, all I said was "sure."

Nick was scary, but he wasn't evil. He was tough, but he wasn't mean. Not many other people could see that. Our friendship grew stronger throughout the remainder of high school. I felt bad about going to university and leaving him behind. I knew he'd take care of the neighborhood and watch over my brothers and my family.

It's amazing how true friends can reconnect immediately. I probably hadn't talked to him in about six months. When I told him what happened to me, his only response was, "What can I do?"

I told him that I had to sort a few more things out at school and that I may need him later on. He didn't express it, but I knew he was furious. So now I had Kevin and Nick on board. These two guys would be all the help I needed to exact my revenge.

My only hesitation was that I was healthy again. I had recovered. I could just let it go. I could just move on. But a flicker of the desire was still burning. I wanted revenge. I wanted to do my homework and do it right. I wanted to be methodical, clinical. I knew the original act so often goes unnoticed while the retaliation gets punished. What if the retaliation is a separate action all in itself? I had the desire and I had ideas about what I wanted to do. But it would be that much sweeter if I planned it in the finest of detail. It would be my extracurricular project for the rest of the term.

The third thing I did at home was make a chart of all the features I remembered about the first two guys. Now that I was heading back to school, it was time to get some more information from Joey. She had said she knew what the first two guys looked like. With luck, the images would still be crisp in her mind. My vision, combined with her memory, should ensure an accurate portrait.

* * *

When I get back to my apartment, the first thing I see is the note I left for myself: "Don't Stay Noble." Don't forgive. It's a beautiful reminder. I leave it up. I finish unpacking and turn on my computer to check Facebook. It occurs to me that I may accidentally come across a photograph of my two attackers. It isn't impossible.

Now that I'm back at school, I can really get down to business. I ask Joey about the guys. At first she's reluctant, but she ends up giving in and providing the descriptions I want. After some hesitation, I let her know that I'm still thinking about revenge. She's not pleased with the prospect, but I feel that in a way she wants some revenge of her own.

Now I have pretty accurate descriptions of what the first two guys look like. I even draw two little pictures to supplement my written accounts. I've never really been a talented artist, but I'm impressed with my sketches. I make a decision then and there that I'll go after these two guys only. Not that I'm an expert with revenge, but I know that, in anything, being greedy is bad. Too many moving parts and pieces can create problems. I don't want to get caught. I choose to believe in my heart that fate will take care of the other four for what they did.

It's good to be back at school with a clear head and no pain. There are scars on my ears and one on my lip that will never go away, but for now I welcome them as reminders.

There's no doubt this small university community will be the biggest help with my revenge. Those two guys are probably starting to forget what they did. They're probably getting comfortable again, not worrying about a knock on the door from the police. The more they carry on with their normal routines, the more the scales get tipped in my favor. The element of surprise is what I'll need to be successful, and that's going to take some time. I'll use that time to better prepare myself, and when I'm ready, I'll have two loyal soldiers at my disposal. I'll take my time and strike back when I'm in a position of strength. Impulsive actions lead to problems.

Like anyone with sinister thoughts, I'm still weighing the consequences. It's over. What's done is done. I'm starting to feel like myself again. The shockwave sent through my world is beginning to settle. But there's no lesson to learn; there's nothing positive to take from what happened. There's no silver lining. My decision is made. Revenge is what I want. It's what I need for my own peace of mind.

There'll be no doubt about this premeditated act of revenge. If the police are called to the scene of my violent actions against these two cowards, they'll just smile, knowing the violence was warranted. They'll get that extra cup of coffee and donut knowing that a civilian took care of his own interest — of his own justice.

It's strange how "I'm going to kill you" has become a common expression. In hockey you hear people say, after a good open-ice hit, "You killed that guy." Originally, I wanted to kill. But murder is unrealistic. Extreme violence is what they deserve. I want to make them remember. I want it to haunt them for the rest of their lives. For Departed One, I'm going to take a large blade and cut both his Achilles tendons. For Departed Two, I'm going to cut two scars on his face that he'll never be rid of. They'll know that their one savage beating of another human being was not worth a lifetime of psychological and physical discomfort. Good riddance.

My recovery is complete. My training's going well. This is only just the beginning. Giving in to the devil on my shoulder and the darkness in my heart feels refreshing. I'm not going to be just another victim. I'm going to stand over them and smile at their agony. For Joey. For me. For anyone who has ever been taken advantage of, beaten down, or hurt.

My dad would be proud. We talked briefly when I was home about what should be done to my attackers. His ideas were just as ruthless as mine. He had a good perspective on what they deserved.

"Kicking a man when he's unconscious and defenseless is unacceptable," he said. "I'd take a baseball bat to their kneecaps and give them a limp they'll never lose."

Good idea, Dad. But I have my own methods. Right now, nothing else matters. I'm going *Kill Bill* on them. I am *The Outlaw Josey Wales*. I'm going to go after them. I can't fight the ...

PART 2
DESIRE

TIME

6

Whoever said time heals all wounds was partly correct. There's nothing like distance to initiate peace. When confronted with a painful situation, it's usually best to simply remove yourself. But what if the painful situation lives on in your mind? How do you remove yourself then? Where do you go?

The easy answer is therapy. My mother made the appointment, which became appointments. She insisted. I would never say it, but the sessions were actually quite beneficial. At first I was guarded and kept my cards close to my chest about the whole situation, pretending I was fine. But it soon came out that I wasn't fine. Even though I wasn't really thinking about what happened to me, it was still there. The therapist recognized that I still had a weight on my shoulders. I still had a lingering feeling that I would run into my attackers. I felt as if everyone I passed on the street either knew about or was connected to the event.

This must be how an escaped convict feels as he operates on the outside, trying to blend in. He feels as if anyone can look in his eyes and see what's on his mind. But this is mostly in his head.

It certainly is all in my head. Other people are just going about their own affairs. They're not paying attention; they're too busy with their own lives.

And time has passed. Like my injuries and the gossip about my assault, the weight has slowly lifted. Joey and I haven't even talked about what happened in at least a couple of months. Life goes on.

However, I find myself habitually staring at faces, analyzing them for any detail that might trigger a memory. Maybe it's a defense mechanism. I suddenly have a great capacity for remembering facial details. I can recognize friends from a block away. This talent is especially useful when I want to avoid awkward encounters. Without really being aware of it, I'm looking for something that matches my written descriptions and drawings. But there's nothing. Life wants to go on.

I'm even making time for my fixation on pop culture again. Life goes on in the celebrity world, too — but not for me. I'm the only one of my friends who hasn't forgotten what Chris Brown did to Rihanna. The media gave his attack on her its fifteen minutes and then moved on. I was outraged. I wanted justice. I wanted Jay-Z to fight Chris Brown for what he did. Eve was the only celebrity who spoke out against him. I don't know Rihanna. I enjoy most of her music, but I'm in no way a super fan. I just couldn't believe that the world would let Chris Brown off the hook so easily. You might argue that he didn't get off the hook. He went to court and did all the courses and seemed repentant. Really?

The harsh reality is that violence happens every day and is simply passed over. Rihanna's case was put under the microscope only because she's a celebrity, and then only for a short time. I'm shocked at how ready society is to sweep behavior like that under the carpet of acceptable celebrity behavior.

For the longest time, I wanted to become a police officer so I could combat domestic abuse. Some things should not be permitted. Some things deserve to be atoned.

The part of me that's reasonable is ready to move on like the rest of the world. But although time has passed, the attack still lingers in my mind, like the last ember in a fire. As Ozzy said, "It's the same old desire . . . burning like fire." No amount of therapy can ever extinguish that.

I'm surprised that I haven't run into them. I'm starting to second-guess the descriptions I wrote down; their sharpness and detail are beginning to fade.

Time is giving me perspective on a couple of things.

The first is how fast things can change. One day, I was walking down the street, not really minding my own business, and the next day, I was waking up in the hospital.

The second is how fast things can go back to normal. I'd call it only about a month before normal life reasserted itself for me. Everything, except my state of mind, is exactly as it was before. That's what the therapist said was best, to let things go back to the way they were, to accept what happened and get back into my normal routine.

But only so far. I'm intentionally letting my desire for revenge consume me. Like a drowning victim fighting for that last breath, I'm inhaling the water and making a vow of revenge. I have reminders everywhere: the scars on my face and the self-made slogan on my wall, neither of which are particularly noticeable to others. Joey and Kevin are the only people who seem to be aware of both.

I'm what many people would call lucky. But I don't feel that way. Time has let things go back to the way they were. But something is different inside me. Something has changed forever. Maybe it's losing that last bit of innocence. Maybe it's the disappearance of that last hope I had for humanity. There's a void there now, and I'm filling it with "impending revenge."

People say revenge doesn't solve anything; they say it makes things worse. To me that sounds like something you would find in a fortune cookie. It may be true, but I want to find out for myself.

There's nothing I want more than revenge. But it's hard to keep your blood boiling for a long period of time. The nitroglycerin in your veins eventually evaporates. You have to keep the memory and the reminders fresh to trigger those feelings again. That's why a coach reminds his team about a previous game with the opponents they're about to face. The past is powerful.

Whenever the light in the mirror catches my scars a certain way, whenever I come home from a long day at class to see "Don't Stay Noble" on my wall, that indescribable feeling of hatred and evil returns. I could buy scar-removal products. I could take the poster down. I could continue with my life. Things are quiet now. I know I'm only one of many victims, and that I shouldn't focus so much on myself. It happens every day.

But that's no consolation. It doesn't happen to *me* every day. I'm a university student with a good heart, a great family, and a beautiful girlfriend. I'm of value. But who gets and deserves value?

Why do some crimes get attention and others fade away? Is it because of who the victim is?

The reality, whether people admit it or not, is that society decides what's valuable. That's why some people love money so much. It's simple. If something's worth a lot of money, it has great value. How do you put a price on revenge? What would it cost for me to fulfill my desire?

What I plan to do to my attackers when I track them down will certainly land me in prison. Lou Reed says, "You're going to reap just what you sow." I lean more to what Billy Idol says: "Enjoy the crime, do your time." In grade eleven law we learned that *mens rea* means "guilty mind." "But officer, they hurt me first" is not an acceptable defense.

If *Boyz n the Hood* taught me anything, it is that revenge doesn't work because there's always someone connected to what happens who will object. They beat me up, so I beat them up. But then someone else beats me up for beating them up. In a way, it ends only when someone becomes a permanent victim. I'm not going to be a permanent victim. I don't want to act irrationally. I don't want my actions to be a reaction. That's why I'm waiting. Time is on my side.

On the other hand, although revenge can wait, in one way time *is* becoming my enemy. I second-guess my intentions daily. Am I waiting to really focus on finding the two guys because I want things to cool down, or because subconsciously I really don't want revenge? I haven't really made an effort to find them, and with every passing day I feel they're slipping farther away.

Maybe I'll never find them. Then what? Am I going back to

being a victim and not an instigator? Despite all my thinking, despite all my weighing of consequences, I have no new developments in identifying the two guys. My training regimen is keeping me fit, occupied, and focused, but I'm a detective with no leads. I'm Elliot Ness with no booze.

I haven't really dealt with that possibility of never finding them. I think about the movie *Memento*. The main character's target for revenge might not have been connected to the event that provoked it. Do my victims really need to be the same two guys that hurt me? Certainly I could project my hatred and revenge on two other bad people and feel just as good as if I'd tracked down the real guys. Maybe my desire for revenge just needs an outlet.

No, it has to be them. I have to hold myself to at least that standard. I'm the good guy. I'm the one with the silver spurs. Which doesn't change the fact that the revenge is weighing heavily on my mind.

The therapy soothes some of my emotional scars but seems to actually motivate me further. Having to say out loud that I got my ass kicked only fuels my rage. The therapy opens my eyes to the impact the attack is having on my life. I have no delusions. Things between Joey and me aren't the same. She saw everything. Couldn't she have done something? I've tried to restore things to the way they were. My attackers have robbed me of most of my dignity. I won't let them rob me of her.

I try to take inventory of all the things that have changed since it happened without me really noticing.

It may sound primitive, but I'm not listening to music anymore. Before, I listened to music everywhere: getting up in the morning, walking to class, studying, making dinner. It made me happy. There's nothing like a song to make you feel better. As The Offspring says, "Music soothes the savage beast."

My tolerance for viewing theatrical violence has changed, too. Even when it's the good guy violently disposing of the villain, a part of me feels sick. Given that one of my favorite scenes in Quentin Tarantino's film *Reservoir Dogs* is Mr. Blonde torturing a cop to the unmistakable sound of Stealers Wheel, this is a problem. The violence was easily dismissed as fake before, but now it seems more real than ever.

The more I think about it, the more it starts to feel that everything has changed. My perspective has been altered. Maybe it was being knocked unconscious. I've lost parts of my identity, parts I dearly want back.

My initial impulse for revenge has faded; now my motivation is different — it's deeper, maybe even more sinister. Now it's not the fact that they threatened my survival but that they've changed my personality. My knot of revenge has been replaced with a steel chain. My desire has never been stronger. But will it be fulfilled? I have to believe it will be. Something has to give. The scales eventually have to tilt in my favor.

I've learned to deal with all the questions about fate that had flooded me in the early weeks. What if Joey and I had walked down a different street that night? What if I had swallowed some pride and kept walking, avoiding the confrontation? These "what if" questions were poisonous.

Now new questions replace the old questions about fate. Am I the same tough, loyal guy I thought I was before? If I have changed in so many ways, do people think of me differently? Everyone says they don't care what other people think about them, but that's never entirely true. People do care. For me, as for most people, it depends on the person. Some opinions I value and some I don't. Even when you think you don't care, what people think can affect you at a subconscious level.

Think of when you're walking down the street and somebody drives by you, yelling, "You suck." Like most people, you're just surprised at first. How can the remark have meaning when the speaker doesn't know you? But then, as the car fades into the distance, you start to think *maybe I do suck.* This sort of thing can ruin your day. Anyone who says they don't care what other people think is lying.

People say you get most of your identity from your friends and family. You're a reflection of them. After reconnecting with my family during my recovery, the only friends I am in contact with are Nick and Kevin. Nick calls me weekly to ask when we were going to get the guys, and Kevin is keeping tabs on me, too.

I need to get back out into the world. I'm not afraid of going out with my friends, but I've been avoiding it. I've been preoccupied with what other people are thinking. The fact is, I haven't really spent time with my friends since it happened. I don't want to talk about the beating. I'll have to squash any attempts to rehash what happened. But real friends are understanding. Maybe it's time to get their perspective. I hope they can help me sort out how I've changed.

Most people have more than one group of friends. Occasionally on big nights, or at big events, you can get the friend groups crossing over. This can be a lot of fun. I'm not looking for anything like that. Baby steps first, right? I'm lucky to have a good group of hometown friends at school with me. It's undeniably my closest friend group and consists of six guys: Tom, Jamie, Jack, Teddy, Will, and, of course, Kevin. They're all unique guys and bring different things to the table. One thing that's distinctive about our group is that we're all physically large. Not one of us is shorter than six feet. We somehow got the nickname The Alpha Males around campus. We pretend to find the nickname embarrassing, but secretly we love it.

They are all great guys and know how to have a good time, so to speak, especially Teddy. Everyone has that one friend who's way out there, and ours is Teddy. He's also full of great ideas. One night he tried to convince all of us to get tattoos of a crescent moon on our asses. He thought it was a hilarious concept. We tried to be nice and shut his idea down while still seeming enthusiastic. Even in small school towns, there's always a tattoo parlor. A visit seems like a great idea when you're drunk, but it can be another thing when you're sober. They don't help by having late hours either. Teddy ended up going there lone wolf that night, getting his desired moon right on his left ass cheek.

The latest rumor I've heard about Teddy is that he got so drunk one night he stood up and pissed on his laptop, frying the hard drive. I miss him. I miss all the guys. It isn't that I want to go out and paint the town. I just need some time with my . . .

FRIENDS

7 There's nothing like friends to remind you who you were, which is not necessarily who you are now. Change is organic. It happens without our really knowing it. When I graduated from high school, I thought I knew everything about everything. Now I can look back and can officially say that I was full of shit. It makes me nervous about my current assumptions. Will I look back in four more years and realize that I'm not so clever now as well? I guess that's part of life. Trying to make things right.

Friends are the foundation of a lot of your knowledge of the outside world. A group of friends is like a democracy. Members of the group may have differing opinions, but they still come to a consensus. On hearing that I want to see them, all the fellas are thrilled. It's not like guys to show a lot of emotion, but I can tell they're happy to see me. It's nice to be wanted. It makes you feel like you have a purpose. Teddy is especially excited, but I think it's because it gives him an excuse to party. I'll take it.

Walking to the bar, I feel nervous. Am I anxious about hanging out with my own friends? The beating has really taken its toll.

But once we're inside the bar, it's just like old times. Hugs are exchanged, and beers are poured. Each of the guys makes the same two remarks at different points in the night: "You look great," meaning that I didn't before, and "If I could get my hands on the guys who did that to you . . ."

Teddy, as expected, gets the most out of hand. Some things never change. Apart from a few casual comments, there are no serious conversations about what happened to me. Everyone seems to feel I've moved on.

Kevin never really leaves my side the whole night. He stays close like a hired security guard. It's nice, but unnecessary. However, it does reassure me that he hasn't forgotten about the state I was in. That's comforting, considering that I'm hoping that he'll help me exact revenge when the time comes.

Kevin's a smart guy, and good friends have instincts. They can tell when something's not right with another friend. And, unlike the other guys, I think he has the feeling that this whole thing isn't completely over for me.

By last call, we've all bought several rounds and have bloodshot eyes worthy of a Visine ad. I realize that I'm especially under the influence because I haven't been out with the boys in some time. Like all inebriated insights, this one seems profound.

At first I'm surprised by the level of enthusiasm and quickly gave myself credit. It's a celebration. A celebration for me. I'm back with my friends, back where I belong. No one can hurt us. We're together and strong, looking out for one another.

If it had been these guys walking home with me that night and not Joey, it would have never happened to me. I'm pretty sure that even just one of these guys would have put the odds back in my favor that night. It's a funny thing to think, on a night when all of them are drunk and acting juvenile, that my friends are reasonable. But it's true: They would have seen the bad situation a mile away and avoided it.

The night is going perfectly. It's accomplishing exactly what I wanted it to — a restoration of personality. But life has a way of reminding us, at the most inopportune times, that things are not fair and nothing is perfect. Like a sports star getting injured in the middle of the playoffs, sometimes things happen that bring everything back into focus.

The boys and I leave the bar early to get some fast food before heading home. Eating cheeseburgers before going to sleep is not the healthiest thing, I'm told, but it does help reduce the next day's hangover.

To say we're all drunk is an understatement. We collectively smell like the inside of a keg. We're all standing in line, too dazzled by the dollar menu to converse, when all of a sudden a guy, who's drunker than all of us combined, cuts in front of us.

Teddy doesn't care about the guy's fragile state. "Hey man, there's a line!" he says.

Everyone's radar is now on high alert. Teddy could've just let it be, but he didn't. The guy slowly turns around, and, without a word, punches Teddy in the face. To give Teddy credit, he keeps his balance pretty well. Instantly all of the boys react and jump on the guy. I can only stand there taking in the whole scene. The reality of it is sobering me up.

The boys pull him outside; they're not finished with him yet.

I don't know whether they're trying to prove a point to me, but they proceed to beat this guy. He doesn't stand a chance. He's trying to swing, struggling to fight, but his situation keeps getting worse. He's in quicksand. Tom punches him right in the nose, and, judging by the explosion of blood that comes from his nostrils, breaks it.

I don't stop them. I don't intervene. I don't even say anything. I let my friends become the same people who attacked me. There's no difference. The results are the same.

Once the guy seems to be unconscious, the boys stop. And just like that, smiles are restored and we begin the walk home.

I'm shocked. It was like my first time watching *Vanilla Sky*. I didn't really know what happened, but minutes later it's all I can think about. I've just watched my friends put a guy in the hospital without even batting an eye, like it was nothing. Where did this rage come from? Why did this violence manifest itself? My friends aren't violent people. They know the concept of a fair fight. But for some reason, they chose to ignore it. They could have defused the situation but chose to lash out instead.

Something is wrong here. I think about the guy. He'll most likely wake up in the hospital just like I did. What's going on? The hate that poured out of my friends astonishes me, but not as much as my change in perspective. Before my attack, I was just like them. I would have been right next to Tom beating that kid's face till it looked like hamburger meat.

I've seen the first silver lining in what happened to me. I'm no longer desensitized to violence. Empathy is back in my life. I'll probably never be able to watch violence in movies the same way again. But where was empathy before? Who was I before?

After we walk about a block away from the burger joint, Jamie looks at me and says, "How 'bout that, eh?"

That sets me off. "I gotta take a leak," I tell the guys, then duck into a nearby alley.

I pull out my cell phone and dial 9-1-1.

"9-1-1, what is your emergency?" the operator says.

9-1-1 is a really crazy concept, if you think about it. But this is no time for philosophy — I have to do something.

"Hi. I was driving past the McDonald's on William Street, and I think I saw a guy unconscious and bleeding there. He looks like he needs help."

I didn't wait for anything else. I hung up the phone. Now the cops have my phone number. They'll come looking for me to ask questions about the incident. I may have just got us into a lot of trouble. But I think I did the right thing. I had to. I had to absolve some guilt. I may have saved that kid's life.

I walk back to the guys. Kevin is waiting for me. Although he'd participated in what just happened, he looks the most shaken up other than me.

"Thanks for waiting," I say.

"Do you think we should call an ambulance?"

I almost smile. "Someone will."

"I'm sorry. That was probably the last thing you wanted to have happen on your first night back out with the boys."

I want to ask why it had to happen. But I don't. I don't say anything. I just want to get back to where Kevin and I live and go to sleep. Who did we think we were, beating up anyone that messes with us, *The Outsiders*? We're all well-off kids whose only concept of violence is from movies and the hockey rink. I'm not trying to write a sociology essay, I just don't get it. When the shoe is on the other foot, it's easy to do nothing. Watching that kid get beaten, I was watching myself. Maybe he deserved it more than me, but what's the difference? I'd just participated in something similar to what happened to me. I continued the cycle. I was part of the problem. The clarity I was hoping to gain by going out with my friends was not achieved.

We weren't Bloods or Crips fighting to survive in South Central Los Angeles. We didn't live on the edge. I guess having every advantage can be boring. If my friends or I came across a card-carrying certified thug, we wouldn't stand a chance. Every male at some point in his life may get the urge to test his knuckles, but violence seemed to be following me. It was tainting even the most harmless of social ventures. Rules and laws had been passed to protect us against violence.

Teddy was quoted later as saying, "I didn't want to back down."

Who does Teddy think he is, Al Capone? No. He's a university student with book smarts and mild alcoholic tendencies. He's not a tough guy. Primitively speaking, we're just a bunch of angry kids looking for a reason to be violent. If deciding not to engage in a violent exchange with another human being over something trivial is considered "backing down," what kind of society are we living in? It may sound wimpy, but what the hell. I'm not a pacifist. Even pacifists permit the use of violence for self-defense or delegated defense. Would you call Muhammad Ali a pacifist?

If it's soft to back down from a fight, it's no less cowardly to beat another human being when it's not a fair fight. Maybe that's the human condition. Kick them when they're down. Get yours because if the steel-toed boot were on the other foot, they'd do the same to you.

These situations are nothing new at this university. Three years ago, a twenty-three-year-old was stabbed to death in one of the most crowded bars near campus. The victim was standing with his girlfriend when his killer approached them. The killer thought the victim had thrown ice at him. After a short argument, the killer pulled out a knife and stabbed him in the chest and then the throat. He bled to death right there on the floor. Maybe he didn't even get a chance to back down.

I'm sure his family doesn't care about the details. They lost a son. Sure, there was a narrative, a story, but we need to focus a little more on the outcome. The outcome was that a young man, with his whole future ahead of him, was killed. That's it. Does somebody have to die for the incident to get any attention? Do the police really have other things to worry about? In situations that are out of control, accidents eventually will happen. When you engage in violence of any kind, anything can happen. Ask the kids who were play-wrestling in the back yard right after they accidentally broke their friend's neck. Results often land far from intentions.

The world isn't Smurf Village where everyone gets along with each other. But to me, this is unnecessary and senseless violence. Even bear cubs and dogs know how to play-fight, and these are creatures we humans feel superior to.

It's not about avoiding risks; it's about managing your life. Listen, if you want to live a completely safe and sterile life, buy a bubble. The world is the world, and I understand that now more than ever. However, these situations all seemed preventable. That young guy getting knifed, my beating, and the most recent beating of that stranger, all of them were preventable in some way. My friends had failed me. They couldn't show me that mine was an isolated incident, that I was just a statistic in the long list of violent crimes that happen every night. And for what? Machismo? Reputation protection? Who cares? The whole thing seemed like one big overreaction. Life goes on.

My lust for revenge takes a severe hit after I watched my friends beat that kid. If I retaliate against my attackers, I'll just be adding to the problem, I think. But I want it so badly. I've built it up in my mind. I've visualized what I will do to them if I ever find them. I want to teach those two guys a lesson. If the cops couldn't prevent them from doing what they did again, I will. I'm trying to be logical and sensible. And some things just have to be done. My action won't be a random act of violence, even if that's the easiest way to get away with it. Mine will be premeditated.

Later that night, I realize that I'll never forget the face of the guy my friends jumped. I'm as guilty as they are. I didn't stop it. To me, the indifference of good people is one of the biggest faults of society. I just stood there and watched. What was stopping him from coming after us, getting revenge on my friends and me? Everyone thinks they're right. Everyone believes that their side of the story is the one worth telling. It would be tough to convince that kid that coming after us wasn't justified.

I feel the same depression and embarrassment I felt after my attack. A helpless feeling. All I want is to rewind time and change what happened. I'm not getting to sleep any time soon. It's nearly four in the morning when I hear two gentle knocks on my bedroom door. Whoever it is wants to know if I'm still awake but doesn't want to wake me up if I'm asleep. It must be Kevin. I don't know any of my other housemates well enough for a late-night wake-up call. I answer my door, pretending to be groggy.

Kevin lifts up a bottle of whisky and says, "Wanna drink with me in the kitchen?"

We head downstairs.

"I'm sorry that had to happen tonight," Kevin says. "You know the boys. Sometimes they get carried away. And the alcohol definitely didn't help."

He puts several ice cubes into two medium-sized glasses and pours the whisky. He slides my glass across the kitchen table. I take a sip before responding. "Yeah . . . It was just not needed. We were in no rush — so what if that guy butted in front of Teddy? We had nowhere to be."

Kevin takes a long sip. His face is expressionless. "I agree. There's a fine line between being a doormat and realizing that it just isn't worth it."

He pauses to take another sip but instead puts down the glass and looks me straight in the eye. He isn't sober, but he understands what he's saying. "I'm sorry for what happened to you. Nobody deserves that. Especially in front of Joey. That must have been awful for her. Those guys are scum."

His words are piercing. He wants my revenge as much as I do.

"Do you ever think about it?" he asks. "I mean, it's been a little while, but do you ever want to find the guys?"

His calm fury brings my desire for revenge to life. It's my turn to be serious. I want to choose my words carefully. Kevin has not forgotten. He still has the motivation. But it's up to me to pick the right time to ask for his help.

"I think about it every day." I take a long slug of whisky. "I still want to find them, Kevin, and I *am* going to find them."

He doesn't seem surprised. He smiles, finishes his whisky, and says, "When you do, you know where I live."

He leaves me sitting alone in the kitchen. I finish the half glass of whisky I have left, dump the ice cubes, and head upstairs with the hope of finding some peaceful sleep. It is comforting to know that Kevin, and Nick, are soldiers to deploy when I'm ready. I don't even look at the clock as I get into bed for the second time that morning. I smile, then shut my eyes tightly, hoping to be rescued by sleep. I feel the whisky taking me on a roller-coaster ride. Not enough to make me sick, but just enough to remind me of one of my favorite Supertramp songs . . .

DREAMER

8 Walking around the Great Cats section of the zoo, I stumble across an incredible lion. The only thing that separates us is a rope, which doesn't strike me as unsafe. He paces back and forth, shaking his mane. What a symbol of power. It must be an embarrassment to this powerful being that I associate him most with a Disney movie. He looks wise, but he also looks broken. His eyes tell me that, like a prisoner in the correctional system, his life in captivity has hardened him. He remembers what it was like to be free. The past weighs heavily on his mind. But these memories are the only things that keep him alive, the only things that keep him strutting around this roped-in enclosure with pride. At least he gets conjugal visits; lions mate very well in captivity.

I walk closer to the rope, which the lion immediately notices. Maybe it isn't such a good idea to get so close. He begins walking toward me. His powerful shoulders and piercing eyes should frighten me, but instead they remind me that I'm only human. He could kill me and eat me and still have time for tea. But this lion looks as if he has something to say or some wisdom to impart. He tells me to pay attention by letting out a roar that blows my hair back like one of those old Maxell tape ads. But he's not finished yet.

In a calming, confident, powerful, slightly Irish voice, the lion says to me, "When a man is getting better, he understands more and more clearly the evil that is still left in him."

Aslan? I have to free him. I've got to find a way to cut the ropes or tell him he can just walk under them. Maybe he doesn't want to be free. Maybe he has chosen to be a prisoner. Just as my heart sinks, a man in a fedora runs up to me. He grabs me by the arm and pulls me away from the lion. He's dressed like one of the backup dancers in Michael Jackson's "Smooth Criminal" music video.

Now we're in an old car and driving fast, even though we're not chasing anyone. I now wear a fedora, too.

"Your gun is in the back," the man says.

My gun? I look in the back seat to find an old-fashioned Tommy gun. What am I going to use this for? I pick it up and feel comfortable with it, even though I've never held or shot a gun in my life. I'm ready to use it for any cause the man needs me to. I feel a loyalty to him, even though I've just met him.

He pulls the car over to the side of the road. We begin to sprint up the road, then he pushes me into some bushes. We conceal ourselves in the shrubs, and I see that he is carrying a Tommy gun, too. It occurs to me we are on a hit. We are about to kill someone. But who?

I ask the man, "Do they deserve it?"

He nods and gives me an authoritative yes.

I guess that's good enough for me. In any case, it seems I don't have much choice. I hear a car approaching. Could this be our target? It's difficult to see through the bushes; I'll wait for my partner to take action. Judging by the noise of the engine and the flashes I see through the leaves, it's another old car. The car pulls over right in front of us. This has to be our target.

"I'll take the woman, and you take the man," my partner says.

What? We're about to murder *two* people, and one of them is a woman? I don't want any part of this. I think about running but realize that might make me a target. I'm frozen. Our first target, the man, gets out of the car. I see the woman sitting in the car.

"Are you prepared to do what needs to be done?" my partner whispers. "Are you prepared to do what's right?"

I don't respond.

Some birds flying overhead distract our male target. Then, without warning, my partner opens fire. The loud noise of the first shot startles me, and I begin to fire. I aim at the male figure. The gun is powerful and loud, but I hear the bullets rip into his flesh. I see pockets of blood shooting out from every wound. The scattering of Thompson bullets makes marksmanship unnecessary. But, judging by the number of bullets that hit my target, my accuracy was never in question.

My partner and I both empty a full clip of ammo into our victims, even after they have hit the ground and are obviously dead. Running out of bullets just seems like a natural ending point for my partner. Judging by his ruthlessness, I half expect him to reload and continue shooting. But he doesn't. They are dead. We've completed our objective. There's no ringing in my ears after the shooting, just silence. My partner begins to walk toward the bodies. I follow. The old car has so many bullet holes, it looks like a strainer.

"We did it," my partner exclaims. "We got Bonnie and Clyde."

I look at their faces to confirm that I have, in fact, just gunned down Warren Beatty. His facial features are hard to distinguish because of the carnage inflicted by the bullets. I walk over to the woman, looking for confirmation. Even though the life has been drained from her face, I can see that she is Faye Dunaway. What have we done?

I turn to my partner in shock and disbelief, but he has vanished. I'm alone at the side of a country road with two bullet-riddled corpses. I want to protest, but no one will hear me. I'm alone.

I yell for help, but then decide to run. I see a barn in the distance. I'm in the barn. It's like a banquet hall. Apart from some tables covered with nice white tablecloths, it's relatively empty. The hardwood floor is freshly buffed and ready for dancing. I've never been much of a dancer. The lighting is dim — mood lighting. I find a light switch and flick it on to get more familiar with my surroundings, but nothing changes. I try another switch — still nothing, a dead giveaway that this is a dream. If you're ever unsure whether you're in a dream, try changing the lighting.

My earlier suspicions are confirmed. This is a dream. I usually don't dream after drinking, but I have to blame this on the early-morning whisky. I don't want to interrupt my REM. I'll just go with it. The worst has to be over.

I look down at my Tommy gun, which has become a sword.

But maybe not. The empty room is suddenly flooded with people surrounding me. The setting is crowded and the figures are now in two big groups. I naturally label them group Departed One and group Departed Two. I've never held a sword in my life, but I take what I think is a sword-fighting stance and prepare to fight.

My faceless attackers are about to strike but are interrupted by a loud gunshot that echoes in the hall. I look up to the ceiling in one corner of the room. There is a fully extended scissor lift with a man perched on the platform. He has what looks like a high-caliber sniper rifle. He pauses for a second, as if he wants everyone to register where he is. He points to where he just shot. He has killed three of my estimated twenty enemies in the first group. I see that a few of the tablecloths now have red spots on them. I'm impressed again by the details my mind can conceive. Never underestimate the incredible precision of the subconscious. The splatter patterns seem accurate, probably taken from multiple *CSI* or *Dexter* viewings.

My guardian angel doesn't wait any longer: He opens fire again, the second shot acting as a starter pistol for my enemies to take aggressive action. They charge me. Their efforts are no match for my weapon. They are defenseless. I can kill as many as four with one swing. My attackers are dropping like flies. I'm winning. Amidst the chaos, I notice my guardian angel is not alone. There is another scissor lift in another corner of the room with a second gunman. They are both doing a tremendous job killing off these faceless wannabe assassins. There is blood splatter and brain matter everywhere. I hope they're being careful enough not to hit me. They seem to be good marksmen. Although they seem to be on my side, I'm not sure I fully trust these angelic figures. Not that I have much choice. I have a sword against their guns.

As the last gunshot echoes in the room, making it clear that the last of the forty assailants is dead, I smile. I don't hear the scissor lifts retract, but my murderous guardians are suddenly right in front of me. As predictable as the plot of a rom-com and about as cheesy, I realize the two snipers are Kevin and Nick. I couldn't have done it without their help. My two soldiers.

I want to thank them, but they vanish, just like my accomplice in the killing of Bonnie and Clyde, leaving me alone — this time with a room full of corpses. The loyalty of my two friends has left me in good spirits, and I want to remain in the dream.

I exit the banquet-hall barn, half-heartedly looking for Kevin and Nick, even though I'm pretty certain I won't see them again in this dream. Right in front of the barn is a brand new Aston Martin, the kind the new James Bond drives. Whose car is it? I find keys in the ignition.

Life is a highway, and this is a dream, so I get into the driver's seat and start the car. It's a stick shift. Who would want such a car in automatic anyway? My overwhelming urge to drive this beautiful automobile is thwarted by the fact that, although I've practiced a couple of times, I don't know how to drive stick. I start to doubt myself until I realize "there is no spoon." I regain control. This is a dream. I can do whatever I want. I am Elvis — The King.

I put the car in gear flawlessly and speed off down the open road. I look as if I belong in a lottery commercial. I can see myself from outside my body because this is a dream. It's as if a full-sized mirror is following me. I have sunglasses that actually fit my face and look good on me. This is the stuff that dreams are made of. No pun intended.

The curvy road and impressive handling of the car is a treat. The simple pleasures in life, right? I'm the wheelman. But I can feel my subconscious getting bored and wanting to change tangents. Maybe I should slow down. Who knows where my mind will go next? Car accidents. More people die in car accidents than any other way. They seem to be an evil tool of fate. Honest, innocent people are killed in the thousands simply in transit. How unfair.

Even though I know this is a dream, I want to keep things positive. But as soon as I see a figure waving at the side of the road, I recall that my subconscious is not prone to happy scenarios. I slow right down and pull over beside the man. Some dust is kicked up, so I don't immediately see his face, but as the dust settles, I start to think he looks like Warden Norton from *The Shawshank Redemption*. He looks serious.

"We need your help flipping the switch," he says.

Switch? What switch? I want to ask, but my thought is interrupted as he gets into the car without asking. It's amazing how possessive human beings can become. This is not my car and it's a dream, but I still feel as if I own this Aston. It's mine. Still, I don't protest to the man getting into the car; I await further instructions.

"Drive down the road," he says. "You can't miss the prison."

He is a warden and they want me to execute someone. I won't do it. I can't do it.

"Come on. Joey is waiting."

So much for keeping things positive. This man has just crossed the line.

"Is she all right?" I ask, trying to comfort myself.

"She'll be just fine when this is all over. Now drive."

I put the pedal to the floor. Safety goes out the window, but Warden Norton doesn't seem to mind.

"This is a fine automobile you got here," he says over the roaring engine.

I see the prison. It's close. It looks like Zelda's Castle, which kind of makes me want to play *Zelda.* I no longer feel apprehensive about what is going to happen. If Joey needs something, it will be easy to know what to do. My own anxieties take a back seat if she needs help.

Warden Norton and I drive through the large cast-iron gate of the prison at top speed. If there was a guard or attendant, he either knew we were coming or didn't have time to protest. My dream skips. I'm inside a prison execution-viewing gallery. I look through the glass into the execution room. It's complete with two electric chairs.

Joey is sitting in the gallery. She turns and looks at me. She's happy to see me and smiles. Even though I'm still concerned, I smile back; I can't help it.

"Isn't this great?" she asks.

I don't know what to say. The closest thing I've ever seen to an execution was in *The Green Mile* when J.C. is put to death. This setting appropriately resembles that. I'm still staring at Joey when Warden Norton taps me on the shoulder. "It is time," he says.

Joey stands up and holds me close. "Enjoy it, baby," she says. "You deserve it."

I start to panic. Am I the one being executed? Did I just rush to my own execution? Can I get a death row pardon? I follow Warden Norton into the execution room. He walks over to the corner of the room and starts giving instructions. This reassures me that I will be doing the executing, and not being executed. "Here's the switch," he says. "When they're both strapped in, all you have to do is flip it."

Then everything is illuminated, as if by a flash of lightning. The door to the execution room opens, and my two attackers walk in.

I see their faces. They are scared. I smile. They are followed by Nick and Kevin dressed in police uniforms. Warden Norton pats me on the back and leaves the room. He goes to sit beside Joey in the viewing room. As my two attackers are being strapped in, I ask them their names. They don't respond. So I yell at them.

"Bet you thought you got the drop on me. Bet you thought you'd get away with it. I bet you had a good time beating the shit out of me in front of my girlfriend while I was defenseless and unconscious. I bet you thought you were tough guys. I bet you all had a good laugh about it after. Who's the bull now? Who has the power now? You guys are going to fry, and I'm going to laugh as you do. My screaming laughter is all you'll hear as you transition from this world to hell."

I want this to be real. They're strapped down and helpless, only ten feet away. As Phil Collins sings it, "I've been waiting for this moment for all my life." I want this to be real. But if it can't be real, I can still enjoy it. Nick and Kevin give me a nod. I look into the eyes of my assailants. Both are crying. I study their faces. I'll never forget them. Just before I wake, I flip the switch, condemning them for what they did and sealing their . . .

FATE

9 The world has a funny way of knowing when our guard is down and then reminding us to always keep it up. This is pretty much a constant in anything. If you're expecting or waiting or hoping for something, that thing won't happen. But as soon as you truly in your heart abandon those stagnant emotions, then it seems to happen. It reminds me of that quote from *Swingers* between Rob and Mike. "I mean, at first you're gonna pretend to forget about her. Not call her . . . but then, eventually, you really will forget about her . . . Somehow they know not to come back until you really forget."

I have to believe in fate: It gives me hope. Fate just has a way of knowing. I wonder about all those success stories, those rags to riches stories that everyone loves, where the person says, "I just never gave up." I think that's a lie. I think the person was in the process of giving up and fate noticed and intervened to give them the opportunity they had been wishing for.

People love the "journey" story model. No one wants to hear about someone who is successful only to get more successful.

They also don't like to hear about a loser who keeps losing. Why do you think everyone loves Oprah so much? It can't all be chalked up to hard work. Sometimes you need the combination of luck and talent to even have a sniff at true success. You need a fastball right over the plate. You need to swing at the right time. You need a home run.

* * *

As I walk down to class, the sidewalks are crowded with people. I feel a little bit like a salmon swimming upstream. People have their headphones on and heads down for the most part. I have a good brisk walk on. My muscles are still tight from my last workout. Today is just like any other day. A feeling starts to come over me, a physical stress that I cannot describe but that I imagine a heart attack feels like. My heart starts racing. In a desperate attempt to find answers for my change of physical state, my senses are heightened. My vision is flawless. My hearing is acute.

I start looking for anything around me that could have triggered this anxious feeling. I see them. I see them in person. I see them in person for the first time in four months. They're laughing. They have big smiles on their faces. They look exactly as I tried to remember them. My sketches and descriptions were spot on. They might as well be portraits.

I can hear my pulse in my ears. I can feel my heart in my throat. It's them. I found them. Departed One and Departed Two. In broad daylight. They're walking down the street without a care in the world. I try not to stare. I try not to panic. It must have been the primal urge taking over my body. Fight or flight. The human body can really work itself into a lather when it gets some information it doesn't want. In a daze I choose another F word option other than fight or flight. I follow.

I wait for a few moments after they pass me and then turn around. I keep my distance. Every good television cop drama has taught me that for a good tail to work, you have to keep your distance. I've never been a good actor, but this is my most important audition.

Walking is quite a difficult thing to do when you are paying very close attention to it. My heart races as I follow them around the block. But a joy that I have rarely felt runs through my veins: a feeling of victory, the feeling of being dealt a full house in poker. I am in the driver's seat. They are the road kill.

I wonder for a moment: Am I certain it is them? This notion is immediately dismissed. I am positive it is them. I have never been more certain of anything in my life. No second-guessing. Nature took over and propelled me so that I wouldn't miss them. Not this time. I have to fight the urge to just attack them now. I am so excited, I feel you could fry an egg on the top of my head. I've got them right where I want them.

They don't notice me. They've forgotten about it. They've absolved themselves. Their guard is completely down. This is perfect. This is fate. I follow them right to their house. With all the other students milling about, following them is easy. No stealth required.

I have to fight the urge to call Kevin immediately to end this right here and now in the street in the middle of the day. That would be reckless. I've come too far. That would jeopardize my cause. It wouldn't be the justice I deserve.

As they enter their house, I stand across the street watching with a smirk on my face. I am at peace. The world has shown its balance. The mother of fate has shown her fairness. I have the power now. I stand there outside their house for an extra minute. I allow this suspicious action out of pure joy. I am so consumed with the emotion of revenge, I almost start talking to myself. If anyone had observed me, I'd probably be in the psych ward by now.

I don't even realize, until I calm down, where I am. I'm very close to my own house — only two blocks away. How could I not have seen them? How could they not have landed on my radar once in these four months? They're practically my neighbors. That prospect almost upsets me until I think of the perfect Arnold Schwarzenegger line, "Grant me revenge! And if you do not listen, then to hell with you." I smile.

As I start the short walk back to my house, I briefly entertain the idea of arson. I could burn down their house while they slept. This is me at my worst, at my most sinister, and I know it. I am the devil's tool. I expected I would have these emotions if I found them, but I guess I never really expected to find them. I dream of being outside their house with a high-caliber machine gun and spraying the house with bullets until I am certain every living thing inside is dead. It's all so simple. One day you're just walking down the street. That's how a lot of things are rationalized. One day, there I was, minding my own business when . . .

I feel my pocket vibrating. It's Joey calling. I think about not answering, but I have to tell someone.

I don't even let her speak. "Joey, you'll never guess what just happened. I found them, Joey. I found them. I was just standing out in front of their house."

She's not as excited about this news as I am. "So what does this mean? Are you going to go after them?"

All I can muster is a yes.

"I'm coming over."

She is coming over with a purpose. She's going to try to talk me out of it. She's going to cry and make me promise I won't do anything. I have to be strong, steadfast. I have to tell her that this is something I have to do. I have to make her understand that fate intervened. I have to promise her that I'll be fine; I'm the one holding all the cards now. I can't wait to call Nick. He'll be thrilled. I picture him smiling his crooked smile with a smoke in his mouth.

I enter my house with such delight, I'm almost skipping. I can't believe I found them. I get to my room and put on a good loud song and flop on my bed. I close my eyes and visualize them again as I've done so many times. This time it's more vivid and fresh than ever. Am I ready for this? I stand up and look at myself in the mirror on my wall. I am clearly physically stronger than I was before. I'm in perfect shape to do what I want to do.

I'm on the verge of a joyous frenzy when I feel my phone vibrating again. It's home calling. I almost answer and shout out the great news, but before I do, I realize that they will be less excited than Joey. I still answer.

It's my dad. "Just checking up on you," he says, "seeing how you are doing."

I have to tell him. I'm going to tell him.

"Dad," I say in such a stern way that it almost echoes. "I found them. Just walking down the street. There they were."

The phone is silent. Maybe he doesn't know what I'm talking about. He has no idea what to make of this information. He's probably put the thought of my beating out of his mind over the past four months.

"What are you going to do?"

I don't respond right away. I let him talk.

"Are you going to call the police? Do you still have the number of that detective?"

I cut him off. "Dad, I'm going to go after them."

He processes this information, and in the single most shocking response I've ever had from him, he says, "You have to do what you have to do."

I almost choke on the air in my lungs and cough into my cell phone, but I hear him loud and clear.

"Be careful. Don't take any chances. You have to have a plan."

Is my father Tony Soprano? How can he really be endorsing this?

"They hurt my first-born son and they deserve whatever they get. If that's what you really want. Don't go alone."

"I won't, Dad. I understand. But if this somehow goes bad, I want you to know that I couldn't get past it. I would be haunted by this for the rest of my life."

"Don't act in anger." He sounds a little like a samurai warrior. "Be deliberate; no passion, just action. Do you understand me?"

"I understand."

"I love you, OK? Call me when it's done."

"I will, Dad, don't worry. And don't tell Mom."

I picture my dad at home sitting alone. I start to cry. That's the second time I've cried because of what happened to me, for those of you playing the home game. Almost on cue, Joey comes into my room. I'm not crying violently or anything, but she knows something is wrong, especially given what I just told her on the phone.

"Don't do it. You don't need to do it. It will be for nothing. You are so much better than they are."

I snap back instantly; my tears evaporate. "You know how much I've wanted this," I say. "I can't feel good about myself unless I do this."

"Can't you see that violence doesn't change anything, and if it does, it's only temporary?"

Her comment cuts deep. I'm pretty sure she just quoted Martin Scorsese.

"Look how well you're doing. You're going to graduate soon and all this will be behind you."

"I can't move on. I can't get past it. I think about it every day, Joey."

"I've supported you since we've been together and through all of this, but I can't support this."

I get the feeling that she's going to break up with me. I play defense. "You're going to break up with me at a time I need your support the most."

"If you hurt them, you'll never be the same. *We* will never be the same. I can't support this."

The tears have become contagious. She walks slowly up to me and kisses me. I'm not angry or sad, mostly stunned. She leaves.

The euphoria I felt having found Departed One and Departed Two, coupled with the emptiness I feel now that Joey has left me, is a strange mix. It may sound pathetic, but at this moment, my focus is not on Joey. It's on them. Maybe there was more to Joey breaking up with me than just me officially being able to get my revenge. It's no longer hypothetical; it is real, clear, and present.

I've been distant with Joey. Ever since the beating I've felt the space between us was growing. This is not what I want. I never wanted to lose Joey because of this. She has stuck by me through everything.

But like a horse with blinders on, I can only see what's right in front of me. At first, in a way, I wanted revenge for her. But now there's no denying how selfish my motivation really is. If she doesn't support this, then I guess now would be a good time to leave. I haven't even done anything yet, but Joey can tell that I am serious. And I am.

I'm not heartbroken over her because I have something to distract me. The key to getting over any breakup is distraction, at least at first. Right now I don't have time to wear sweatpants, eat junk food, and sit in front of the television feeling sorry for myself. I have to get the wheels in motion. Enough speculation and reflection; it's time to act. I'm physically ready and as mentally prepared as I could be. I will start by enlisting my soldiers.

I go downstairs to see Kevin. He's watching television but can feel my fire as I enter the room.

"What's up?"

"Remember what we talked about in the kitchen that night?"

His eyes widen.

"I need your help, Kev. I found them. I know it's them, and I know where they live."

He plays dumb to buy time. "What are you talking about?"

"You know exactly what I'm talking about, Kevin. The guys who beat me. They live just around the corner."

"Are you sure?"

"I'm positive,"

He stands up. "I don't know . . . I don't know if I have it in me to just go and attack two strangers."

Well, this is disappointing. Where's all his enthusiasm and tough guy talk now? "You said you'd help me. I would help you."

Kevin really doesn't know how to respond, and I can't blame him. I just came into the room like a tornado. I'm completely juiced.

His participation as a soldier in my revenge seems to be doubtful. "After that night, I gave it a lot of thought. I don't want to be like that anymore. It's just not worth it."

I'm fed up. Why doesn't he understand? All I want to do is get the process started.

"I hope you understand," he says. "I'd do anything for you, but I can't do this."

Who is he, Meat Loaf?

My frustration boils over. "I'm going back upstairs to call Nick, Nick O'Gallagher, 'cause he seems to be the only friend I have with some balls."

As I walk out of the room, I tell him again, "I would help you."

I feel truly alone. This day has been full of surprises. After months of redundancy and nothingness, speculation and over-analysis, it has all come together in a day. And those two pieces of shit have taken two more things from me: Joey and my faith in Kevin. I think about what Kevin said — that it wasn't "worth it." Maybe it does seem that way. But at this point, those two losses just seem like more motivation. None of this was part of the plan. I need some enthusiasm.

I notice my phone vibrating on my desk. The screen reads "N. O'Gallagher." I immediately answer, struggling to maintain composure. "Nick, I've got great news," I say.

"You found them."

I love this guy. "Yeah, I found them. I know where they live and everything."

"All right," he says calmly. "I'll be down this weekend, and we'll take care of them. See you Friday."

Before I can say anything else, he hangs up. He is my all-seeing, all-knowing guardian angel from hell.

* * *

All this is happening so fast. No time at all for reflection, which I admittedly have done too much of in the past months. After this weekend, the biggest puzzle piece of my life will be put in place. The case will be closed and the folder filed away. I will have my revenge.

Like the ending of *The Sixth Sense,* everything is coming together in a flash. My life has just taken some dramatic, violent twists. I'm not sure if I've navigated them in the best way possible, but ain't that life? No horoscope could ever capture what just happened in my day, but in a way it all feels like an act of fate. And my white knight, with brass knuckles and more scars than Rambo, is coming to the rescue with . . .

A PLAN

10 A week of sleepless nights and anticipation makes Nick's knock on my front door a big relief. He hadn't called, and, given all the recent rejections I'd received, I was wondering if he'd even show up. But here he is in my room taking it all in. I'm in good hands. No pleasantries or small talk, just right down to business.

"I got everything we're going to need in my trunk," he says.

I'm glad Nick came prepared, because I suddenly realize how amateur I am at this level of violence and revenge. The only revenge I know is the occasional retort with a friendly prank, nothing of this magnitude. This is serious.

"After it's over, I'm going to drop you off and drive straight home, no discussion. I'd love to stay up here and drink to justice, but that just wouldn't be smart."

All I do is nod. This may be my act of revenge, but it's his show.

"We get a good night's sleep tonight, and then we stake out the front of their house. It could be a while before we get the opportunity we're looking for, which is both of them leaving the house together, preferably at night."

Nick was never the best student, but he sounds like an expert on this topic. I guess he has his Ph.D. in street smarts. You can't put a value on friendship, and I'm not advocating anyone go out and seek criminals as friends, but sometimes you need someone in your corner with little regard for the laws of society. It makes them capable of anything. And I would never describe Nick as a criminal; I would describe him as my friend.

"We have to put them down quickly and make it a point that they stay down. We can't give them any opening or courtesy. Quick and dirty. That's the only way this is going to work. It has to seem like a random act."

The plan is simple. Well, Nick's plan is simple. I'd be lying if I didn't say that I pictured something a little more glamorous. My dramatic desires have to take a back seat. If Nick and I are going to get away with this, we have to be aware of what the outside world will do with it. Real consequences mean no room for error. I have a score to settle, and no one else is playing the game except for Nick.

"One of us should make a point of demanding money so that it looks like a petty robbery. We're not going to have a lot of time with them because we want to limit the number of witnesses."

Witnesses? Nick really has thought of everything. He doesn't want to get caught. We won't get caught.

"After it's over, you'll disappear. Order food, watch movies, lie low. If the cops come a-knocking, you get Kevin to give you a damn good alibi. You think you can do that?"

Then, with a smile, he says, "Any questions?"

I am excited. Although it feels like a lot to digest, the genius is in its simplicity. It's a simple beating; why complicate it? Hit and run. This is going to work. It has to work.

"You got anything to eat in this place?" Nick asks.

"Yeah, downstairs. I don't think anyone else will be cooking."

As Nick and I head to the kitchen, I hear that someone *is* cooking. It's Kevin. This interaction should be awkward — something like, Hi Kevin, you remember Nick, he's agreed to help me with the revenge you wouldn't.

My uneasiness about the coming interaction is confirmed.

"What's Nick doing here?" Kevin says.

Great start.

"That's none of your business, Kev, but nice to see you, too," Nick says.

"Nick," I say, "help yourself to any of my food. It's on the shelf on the left in the cupboard and on the bottom shelf of the fridge."

I continue on to the TV room. Nick and Kevin don't talk, which is probably for the best. I search for some mindless programming. I haven't felt this comfortable in a long while, even though I'm roughly twenty-four hours away from violence. Just having Nick here brings that much more legitimacy and purpose to my desires. It's real. It's going to happen.

Following Nick's instructions, we both retire pretty early. As Nick is making his makeshift bed on my bedroom floor, I'm reminded of the sleepovers we used to have in high school. It has sort of come full circle. He used to sleep on my floor, which was my way of helping him. Now he's still sleeping on my floor, but this time to help me. You can't put a price on this kind of loyalty.

I don't want to get sentimental at all, but I have to ask, "Why are you doing this, Nick? Why help me?"

It's a heavy question that I half expect he will shrug off.

"What a drama queen," he says. "I'm helping you because you're the only person who ever gave a shit about me. Is that simple enough for you? Every day in high school, I used to worry about having a safe place to sleep that night, because I couldn't have safety and comfort at home. You had that, and you shared it with me."

I struggle for an appropriate response. Nick opening up like this is rare. "You know you're part of my family, Nick, and I can't thank you enough for being a loyal friend all these years, even though we don't see each other that much."

"Loyalty beats proximity."

"What, are you writing bumper stickers now?"

"I'm not the one who got all emotional, you pussy. Speaking of which, how's Joey?"

"We broke up."

"Really? She loved you, man."

"I know. I guess she just wants some space."

He must know that she broke up with me as a result of what happened and the person I've become. Talking about it makes living it harder. Regardless, very soon things will be made right. I'm going to set the record straight.

"Well, I'm sure you'll give one of those two guys an extra kick for her tomorrow. She had to go through it with you, maybe not physically, but she had to watch."

"Let's hope I get that opportunity."

"You will, I promise."

He falls asleep almost right after promising revenge. I hope I get lucky and sleep embraces me with ease tonight. I need the rest. I close my eyes and start visualizing, not dreaming, visualizing. I remember a coach advocating visualization as the best preparation for any stressful situation. I think it was for tennis. Picturing yourself there, actually in the moment, can be very helpful. It's like a test run for your senses, and when done right, you can get your heart rate going to around the same speed it will be in the actual situation. This helps make it familiar. Finding comfort in a situation that is out of your comfort zone is ideal. I must be getting more sociopathic if I'm visualizing violence with such ease.

As I am about to visualize my attack on Departed One, I wake up to a knock on my bedroom door. It's already morning. A restful, dreamless, full night's sleep was exactly what I needed. Nick is still on my floor sound asleep. I get the door. It's Kevin.

"What do you want?" I say. I'm all business. This is my big day.

"I want . . . I want to help you guys."

I don't know what to say. I guess he couldn't face himself.

"You don't have to do that, Kevin. I get it. It's not worth it for you."

"Listen, I'm coming to help, whether you guys like it or not. I didn't sleep at all last night. I want to be there. I want to see the look of surprise on their faces."

There's my boy. There's the boy who knocked on my door to help him drink some whisky in the wee hours of the morning. But I'm still going to leave the exit door open to make sure he is sure.

Just as I say, "Come on, Kev, we can handle it," the exit door gets slammed on him.

"We could use him. Numbers always help," Nick says. "Welcome aboard."

Kevin and I shake hands because it just feels like the right thing to do.

"Eat a big breakfast and pack some sandwiches and snacks, boys, 'cause we're staking it out like Starsky and Hutch," Nick says.

After eating a hearty breakfast, the three of us go back upstairs to get ready. We're dressed in black from head to toe and in clothes we're OK with burning after. I pull out a knife and show it to Nick. "Should I bring this?" I ask.

He smiles at me. The kind of smile the devil would applaud. "No. I got everything we need in my trunk . . . Oh, but we're going to need an extra balaclava for Kevin or a mask or something."

I walk over to Kevin's room and give him one last chance to back out. He's listening to David Bowie's "Modern Love." He's nervous. I know him well enough to know that he needs some upbeat music to get his mind off what he's about to do.

"Last chance," I say.

"I know. Let's get 'em," he says holding up a balaclava. He turns the music off and walks past me and down the stairs. It's amazing how human beings will rise to the occasion. No more than a couple of days ago, violence on complete strangers didn't sit well with Kevin. But now he might as well be Marv from *Sin City*.

Nick walks slowly down the stairs and starts a pre-game speech that Pacino in *Any Given Sunday* would be proud of. "This is serious shit. No-turning-back kinda shit, boys. We are going to hurt them. We are going to hospitalize them. This will be an event in their lives they will never forget. The injuries may even stay with them for their entire lives. We have to be ruthless. We have to hit them when they are down, because, as we know, they would do the same to us and anyone else. We want to minimize our time outside, so you guys walk to my car and get in. I'll get our tools out of the trunk and get into the car. You got it? Preferably we will get our chance at night, but this could be over in an hour. Let's get 'em."

We exit the house like a SWAT team. Nick walks quickly to the trunk of his car. Kevin and I follow, almost step for step. I walk around to the front seat, and Kevin gets into the back. It takes only a second for Nick to grab his tools from the trunk. I'm extremely curious about what he has; I can only assume they are weapons. Nick eases into the car and drops a small but heavy cylindrical object in my lap.

"What's this?"

"Never seen an extendo bat before?"

I wouldn't consider myself an expert, but I am familiar with extendo bats. "Familiar" meaning that I've never actually seen one before except on the news being used by cops.

"You just whip it out and it extends into a full baton, like a night stick. That thing will shatter a forearm with little to no effort. Compact and ruthless. Just what we need."

The mere display of extending the baton is psychologically intimidating. Perfect.

"One hit with one of those to the back of the leg, and your man goes down. Think you can handle that?"

"For sure."

"Sorry, Kev," Nick adds, "you are just going to have to bare-hand this one. I only have two of these little bastards and I can't wait to use mine."

The car is a key element of this plan. Without it, we would look like the most suspicious three guys ever. Three guys wearing all black with balaclavas in hand, two of them carrying extendo bats. We'd look like the music video for "Eye of the Tiger" by Survivor. I feel powerful holding the extendo bat. The odds are so much in our favor, I almost feel at ease during the short drive to Departed One and Departed Two's house. The Doors' "Light My Fire" is on the radio as we drive over. It might not be the most appropriate song, but it fills the silence.

Ideally we will just drive over and they will be right there waiting for us, saying, "Take your revenge, we deserve it." Realistically, I feel like we might have a bit of a wait on our hands. Nick said he wanted to get them together, at the same time, which seems logical. So let's hope that their daily routine entails a few activities in common.

My perfect scenario is that Departed One and Departed Two go out to meet some friends for a few drinks. Their guard is down, and visibility is poor. Then we strike. But I expect that it might be in broad daylight with a few bystanders to witness it. Not that I am worried about witnesses, I just feel bad about ruining more than just the intended targets' day.

We arrive at our destination. Nick pulls up to the curb right across the street from the house of Departed One and Departed Two and shuts off the engine. I think Nick purposely chose this way of parking so he can be the one to initiate the violence. He knows Kevin and I are not accustomed to this sort of rage. He flicks the ignition so we can listen to the radio while we wait. I've never been on a stakeout, and I haven't been on a picnic in a very long time. This feels like an odd combination of both.

"All right, boys. Now we wait. We wait for both of them. Don't get excited if one of them comes out solo. That's not what we want. Don't get distracted. Stay alert. They could come out any second. We have to be ready."

He sounds a bit like a tracker or a hunter you might see on the Discovery Channel. I guess in a way we are hunting. None of us really has anything to talk about, so the radio is welcome. The classic rock station we have on has a great playlist.

The radio is a funny thing. Listening to it evokes something like the feeling you get when a movie you already own comes on TV. For some reason, the spontaneous feeling makes you get into it. Despite the obligations you may have, or however cut up by censorship it may be, you watch it. If *Gladiator* had come on before we left today, we would have had to push this back a day. Despite having epic qualities, that movie is basically just a story of revenge. I start to think about some of my favorite scenes to pass the time.

An hour passes. It is almost afternoon. The radio carries us through with relative ease. I notice Nick focus on something. He straightens up in the driver seat. He extends his neck and narrows his eyes. I look at the front door of the house. Departed One and Departed Two are exiting. Led Zeppelin's "Ramble On" comes on; Robert Plant is singing, "Now's the time, the time is now."

This is it, the moment we've all been waiting for. Their short walk down their front steps, into the yard, and out the path is in slow motion. This is perfect, apart from its being in broad daylight. They're together and there are not that many people around. Nick's criminal mind snaps into action.

"We got 'em. Look alive, boys. As soon as they hit the sidewalk and turn their backs, we hit 'em up. You got it?"

No response; we know the score.

The song changes. I recognize it — it's Mick and the boys singing "Get Off of My Cloud." Good soundtrack.

"Don't stare at them. Just wait," Nick says.

It's hard not to stare when they're right there. When you have your target in sight, why would you turn away? It's like asking a tactical sniper to cover his scope.

I think of all those cops on stakeouts gathering information. They're so close to the criminal action, but they're on the outside looking in. They gather evidence for a bust that may or may not happen for a court case that may or may not deliver the correct verdict. Not able to strike, they must feel like a caged lion at the zoo, knowing that, if not for the cage, things would be much different.

They are only ten feet away. They are about to hit the sidewalk and turn the corner. I can feel my pulse beating in my ears. I hold the extendo bat in my hand so tightly that my knuckles turn white and my hands start to sweat. I look over at Nick. He's got his game face on, smiling a smile that all the demons in hell would be proud of.

"Now!" he shouts and we all burst out of the car. We hit the ground running. Any bystander is either in the process of calling the police or running away to call the police. This must look bad. In only four steps we're behind them.

This is it. Time to get my ...

PART 3
REVENGE

ACTION

11 They don't stand a chance. Nick extends his baton and it snaps into place with a haunting click. Departed One hears this and looks over his shoulder. I'll never forget the look on his face. The jig is up, the dice are loaded, the trump card has been played. Seeing his face only adds to the already large dose of adrenaline pumping in my veins.

I whip out my arm and my baton extends with precision. Before Departed One can alert Departed Two, Nick takes a full swing and hits him in the kneecap with the baton. The sound is exactly the same as when Rocky punches frozen meat. A dense thud. The element of surprise doesn't quite describe it. How about the element of total and complete shock?

As Departed One crumbles to the ground in extreme agony, I can see his face searching for answers. Why is this happening to me? He's in so much pain, he has no air in his lungs. Fight or flight? He can't fight and he can't fly. He's mine. I own his life.

Departed Two finally notices his fallen friend and turns just in time for Nick to land his baton right on his forearm. I don't know much about these extendable batons, but I do know they turn bones to butter. Departed Two's right forearm is a wet noodle. His bone matter is sawdust. He joins his friend on the ground.

I start in on Departed One, who has now chosen the fetal position as an appropriate defense. It will do him no good. I want to make sure I say all the things I need to say. I let the extendo bat do the talking for now. It's my first time at bat and I'm swinging at every pitch.

I hit him on the back, going for his ribs. He moves at the last second and I catch one of his kidneys. He yelps in pain. I can see in my peripheral vision that Nick is picking apart Departed Two. My heart is beating so fast I am trembling, but I have to focus on my task. I swing at Departed One's shoulder and connect. I make up my mind I'm going to make this a little more personal once I'm certain he can't fight back. I hit him in the other shoulder with the extendo. We've taken away both his arms and one of his legs. I drop the extendo.

I roll Departed One over and look into his eyes. He's crying. But I'm a demon, and I'm not finished. I aim my fist to the bridge of his nose. I punch him right on the nose, which I'm sure will hurt my hand later on. His eyes well up with more tears and his nostrils explode like water balloons filled with blood.

"Look at me!" I yell. "Look at me! Remember me? How tough are you now? You and your friends were pretty tough. Look at you now! You're pathetic."

I hit him in the chin, which achieves two things. It knocks him out cold and breaks his jaw. I can tell this by the immediate bulge near one of his sideburns. I've just destroyed a human being. The only thing in his immediate future is painkillers and Adam Sandler movies. I've made my point. But I want more. My thirst for violence needs only one more little sip.

I pick up the extendo and go over to Departed Two, who has been disposed of in similarly violent fashion by Nick. I'm shaking, but Nick speaks to me calmly. He must have ice in his veins. "Go through their wallets and take the money," he says.

Before I can ask why, I hear Kevin. "Let's go. We gotta get out of here."

He's right. Kevin and I both run over to the car and get in. I watch from the car as Nick quickly empties their wallets, drops them on their bodies, and sprints to the car. I take one last look at the motionless bodies as the dust settles. I can still hear them whimpering. I smile as Nick puts the car in gear and we drive away. My whole body feels like the end of a blowtorch. There's an indescribable ringing in my ears. The revving of the car's engine is muffled, as if I'm wearing earplugs.

When the blood returns to my brain, I start realizing a few things about what just happened. The first thing is that Kevin didn't participate, not even a little. He got out of the car with the same fury that Nick and I did. He had bad intentions all over his body language. Then he just watched. Now is not the time to bring it up, but I am curious. Maybe it was because he didn't have a weapon. Maybe he was scared or something. We certainly didn't need his physical presence. All I know is that he was the one who called a stop to it. He had a clear enough head to get us to break our concentration. I might have never stopped if he hadn't spoken up. I'm glad he did. I'm glad he came along, even if it was just for moral support. Our friendship would definitely have suffered if he hadn't. I knew he'd come with us. It's like my favorite exchange from *Rounders*:

"Hey, how'd you know I was coming back?"

"That's easy. Who's your favorite actor?"

"Clint Eastwood. *The Outlaw Josey Wales,* man. *The Man with No Name*. He always doubles back for a friend."

That's a good way to describe Kevin.

The second thing I notice in the short car ride home is that Nick didn't even break a sweat. What did I expect? But seriously, he's in the exact same form as before. You'd think he'd be driving with a lead foot after what we just did. But there's nothing. No indicators at all. I'm still shaking, and he is totally cool. I fully expect him to turn to me like Harvey Keitel in *Reservoir Dogs* and say, "Let's go get a taco." In fact, he says, "Where can we go get something to eat? A cheeseburger, I want a cheeseburger. I'm starving."

These are the first words spoken since it happened, and they catch Kevin and me completely off guard. Our thoughts are definitely still back on the street. Nick's mind couldn't be farther away.

All I can think to say is "yeah."

This seemed to me to be a reckless deviation from "the plan." But again, I'm not going to argue with Vincent Vega in the driver's seat. He's calling the shots. He hasn't led me astray so far. I guess if the man wants a cheeseburger after what he's just done for me, he should have it. It would seem logical to get this car off the road, but I could do a cheeseburger, too.

In no time we're at the McDonald's drive-through. We stash the balaclavas under the seat. For some reason I feel like buying ten happy meals, putting together all the toys, and then smashing them. Just because. Right now, no one is safe, nothing is off limits.

You can tell a lot about a person from their order at McDonald's. You have the conservative, delusional consumer. Everyone is aware that eating fast food is bad for you, but this person chooses to try limiting, restricting, and twisting their intake in a futile attempt to "eat healthy." In the end, they usually end up in some way making it worse. They ask for no salt on the fries, then they load up on ketchup. They take a Big Mac, then order a salad. As George Carlin would say, that's like screwing for virginity.

The next up in the fast food chain are the people who are cost-sensitive. They'll get the most food for the least money, even if the sandwich of the day is the one I've never seen ordered, the Filet-o-Fish.

Last, but not least, are the "garburators." These are the people I respect and strive to be like. Their receipt ends up looking like an old scroll. They have to stop themselves from ordering every combo on the menu. They order so much food, their fridge is littered with freezer-burned burgers for a week.

I feel like being a garburator today. I want to feel my blood vessels tighten and my cholesterol rise. I want to breathe smoke and spit fire. Like Dire Straits sings, "My life makes perfect sense. Lust and food and violence."

Talk about projecting. Anything to get my mind off what just happened. Here I am pondering McDonald's personality types. All this has run through my mind and we haven't even ordered yet.

We have to make this quick and get back to the house. The car we're in is pretty common, but that's why they invented license plates. I have to stay calm and focus on my order.

"What do you want?" Nick says.

Here goes: "May I please have three McDoubles, a large fries, a large vanilla milkshake, and a root beer, please."

Nailed it.

"So polite, two pleases. No McFlurry for dessert?" Nick says. He's as cool as can be.

It takes the guy — what do you call them at McDonald's — waiter, server, trough filler? — anyway, it takes him three trips to bring all of our orders. I'm not waiting till we get back to the house. I unwrap my first burger and take a crippling bite. My pupils dilate and my heart skips a beat. I chew twice, breathing a sigh of relief.

Nick is right again. I wouldn't trade this burger right now for a flying DeLorean. To pinpoint it more accurately, it gives me the same emotional rush as an ice-cold beer on a hot summer day. There's nothing better.

Nick pulls the car deep into the driveway near the back of the house, just in case someone "made" the car and a cop cruiser drives down our quiet street. Seems logical. Once we get inside, Nick takes another opportunity to show the true brilliance of his criminal mind.

"We got 'em. They got what they deserved, and you can take comfort in knowing that, fellas. All right. I got a shovel in the trunk of my car. We'll take turns digging two good holes in the back yard. And just so we're all on the same page, one is for a nice little bonfire, and the second one is for the extendos. So we'll dig the dimensions of the holes according to those needs. We'll take shifts and get this done quickly, have a quick celebration, and then I'm out of here, boys."

My hero. Winston Wolf, solving problems. Kevin and I head to the back yard to wait for Nick and his shovel.

The digging doesn't take that long, but I doubt if our landlord will appreciate our yard work. The shift-based hole-digging system is extremely effective. I think we're still a little jacked up from all the violence and McDonald's. Nick shovels the last piece of dirt and deems it enough.

He wipes his brow and says, "We're almost there, boys. Just being precautionary, you know. I'll bury the extendos. You guys build a nice fire — nothing off the set of *Backdraft* where some old lady out walking her poodle is going to notice and call the cops. Just enough to burn our clothes. Once we all change, we'll break out the whisky and celebrate."

Kevin speaks for the first time in a long while. "You really think that's such a good idea, Nick? Should we really be drinking? Shouldn't you hit the road?"

Nick's not even a little fazed. This is his world, and right now Kevin and I are just visiting it.

"Once those extendos are buried and our clothes are burned, that only leaves the car. I'll be leaving first thing in the morning, hopefully not too hung over, and driving straight to the junk yard back home to finish covering all our tracks."

Kevin and I continue to be amazed by how Nick is acting. By no means is his plan flawless, but what plan is? The only thing scarier than watching him today is knowing that it doesn't bother him at all. I feel a little sick to my stomach.

The work is done. The director yells "cut." We change clothes and take our all-black uniforms out back to the bonfire. Since we feel like such bad asses after our criminal day, we're drinking whisky right from the bottle.

Nick is the first to toss his clothes on the fire. He dusts his hands off. As his clothes slowly burn, he takes a big swig of whisky. The three of us don't talk very much. Trying to make small talk seems pointless.

I don't want to talk to Kevin about his lack of participation in front of Nick. I don't want to embarrass him. I know that Nick and Kevin don't really get along, and this bonfire has been the most relaxing part of my life in the last few months. Preserving the calm atmosphere would be nice.

But Nick just can't help himself. He's a tough guy, bordering on crazy, with little tact or social grace. He's been on my side for a long time, the events of this afternoon being a case in point. I had forgetten how ruthless he can be to others.

"Did you get spooked today or something, Kev?" he asks.

I should step in and defuse this. "Come on, Nick. It's over. Let's just relax," I say. "I want to make a toast and thank you both right now. Here's to the two most loyal and tough guys a friend could ask for. You know I'd do anything for you two. Thank you for your help. It means more to me than you'll ever know."

It works. I take a big swig of whisky and then pass it to Kevin who shyly takes a big sip and passes it to Nick.

"I didn't mean anything by it," Nick says. "It was good having you there on lookout. I wasn't questioning your dedication."

Kevin doesn't say anything. Seeing that Nick's clothes have

burnt down, he picks up his clothes and throws them on the fire. It smothers the fire temporarily, but the flames prevail, as they usually do.

"You seen Joey recently?" Kevin asks me.

I take his comment as good-natured, although initially I feel a slight sting. Is he trying to say something more? I feel like asking, "Why do you care?" But I end up saying, "Haven't seen her in a little while. I hope she's doing well."

It sounds a little too fake and scripted, but it's better than shooting down Kevin's attempt to make conversation. The whole situation weighs heavily, but the more we drink, the less we think. I bring up a topic of conversation I know we can all talk about casually: movies — gangster movies.

"Scorsese needs to make another gangster movie," I say.

"No doubt about that," Nick says. "The guy just makes good movies."

"There was some talk that Pacino, Pesci, and DeNiro were working with Scorsese for a crime flick," Kevin says. "I heard that rumor a while ago and it got me excited, but I haven't heard anything since."

"That final scene with like four head shots in *The Departed* was the most shocked at the movies I've been in my life," I say.

"And you know, the actors must trust him," Kevin says. "Like Leo dies in a lot of his movies, but to sign up for an unglorified bullet right between the eyes, you gotta have some faith in your director."

"Casting Ray Liotta as Henry Hill in *Goodfellas* was genius," Nick says.

"Some good gangster movies have been set in Boston recently." I say. "But I can't wait till someone takes it back to NYC. There were some scary Irish mobsters in New York, man."

Our minds drift away from today, and tomorrow is approaching soon. We call it a day. The clothes that needed to be burned are gone, and we were all in that great state of drunken fatigue in which, as soon as you shut your eyes, the movie fades to black.

* * *

After a dreamless sleep, I wake up in my room slightly hung over but with a big grin on my face. I got them. We got them. Justice has been served. The good guys have won, and with Nick's departure coming soon, we will have made ourselves very difficult to connect to the crime.

All Departed One and Departed Two have now is a long recovery and maybe some therapy. They still probably don't know what happened. At least I got to make my point. Whether they remembered me or not, they have to feel some humiliation in knowing that they deserved what they got.

Probably the only thing they feel right now is pain. But I've given them scars that go beyond the flesh. I've carved out a piece of their minds. They'll always remember it. Just as I will always remember when I was beaten.

I take pride in knowing that maybe our assault has given them some kind of a wake-up call. Just what that call was, I haven't quite decided yet. Who knows whether it will change them or not.

I hear Nick yell from downstairs, "OK boys, I'm heading out."

Kevin and I go down to see him off. I don't want him to leave. There's a certain level of comfort when he's around. He's the kind of guy you want in your corner in any situation. Well, maybe not a math exam, but anytime instinct and street smarts are needed.

I shake hands with Nick, which leads into a hug. I can never repay him for what he did for me. His orchestration of my revenge has salvaged some of my dignity and made me the happiest I've been in a long time.

"Boys, take care. If the cops come a-knocking, which they won't, remember they have nothing on you, so be cooperative. Indulge them. I gotta get on the road and get this car to the yard. Take care, and I'll see you guys back in the city."

As he is about to get into the car, I say . . .

GOODBYE, NICK

12 It didn't even occur to me to ask Nick where he got the car he was driving. I figured he had borrowed it from the junkyard or something. He's so confident in every action he takes because he has nothing to lose. If you don't really care about anything, good decisions or bad decisions are pretty close to being the same.

But Mom calls me a couple of days after Nick drives away. Her news shakes me to the core. Nick had been caught by the police driving a stolen car. He's being charged and will probably go to jail. I'm so blown away when I hear that, my soul seems to slip away for an instant.

I don't even put it together until later that the car they picked him up in was the same car we used. He got picked up on the way home. The cops spotted his car and ran the plates.

I expected Mom to say that he resisted and they shot him. But he cooperated and is in custody.

Everything is getting a little too dramatic. I know there's no way for the police to link what happened here to him unless they had found a witness who'd memorized the license plate. If this super witness exists, he's certainly taking his time to come forward.

Now I'm no longer worried about Kevin and me; I'm worried about Nick. We might have gotten away with one crime, but it's a real possibility that he could be going to jail for another. He's an adult now, and that means adult consequences. I can't believe it. His planning was flawless. He did all the hard work. I can't help but feel I should be in jail with him. I feel guilty. I feel as if I owe him my life. I know my parents will do whatever they can to help him, but life isn't like Monopoly, and there are no real get-out-of-jail-free cards. I feel that his getting picked up is my fault. All he was doing was helping me.

My guilt, as it usually does, turns into anger. Why did Nick have to steal a car? How could he have been so stupid? But I have to stop myself. I know Nick. I know my friend. Things were never really that complicated for him. He had a friend in need and needed to get to that friend. Might as well steal a car and just get there faster. As careful as he was, his loyalty blinded him. His loyalty to me.

I would take back what we did if it meant Nick would be free. I would do it in a heartbeat. That sort of friendship and loyalty beats anything.

I know Nick won't say anything to the police about what we did. It's the last thing I would worry about. I make sure to tell Mom and Dad to help him out any way they could and to let him know I'd be down to see him soon.

Nick's dad probably doesn't even care. He probably wouldn't even notice that he was gone. I want to tell Kevin what happened to Nick, but I don't know how. Even though they had made their peace, I'd half expect Kevin to respond that it served Nick right if he stole a car. Or maybe he'd just worry that he might be compromised. He wouldn't get it. I'll tell him later. Maybe there'd be better news by then.

One thing is of some comfort. At least Nick would have an enjoyable memory to get him through whatever time he had to do. His criminal mind could replay the actions we carried out over and over again. I could just picture him sitting there with a big smile on his face knowing that he helped a friend right a wrong.

Nick was in trouble, there was no doubt about that. But if he had to get caught, it was lucky it was for the car. He would just shrug his shoulders and be thankful he hadn't been picked up for the violent crime.

But why couldn't I get my happy ending? All I wanted to hear was that Nick was safe back home doing his usual thing. Kevin and I will be able to carry on our usual routine, but Nick will be in prison.

Having seen all those *Dateline NBC*'s, I start thinking that maybe Nick's time in prison will be good for him. Not likely. Jail is crime college. Nick is going in as a car thief. Who knows what he'd come out as. Would he even be my friend anymore?

I have to believe, for my own sanity, that our bond will hold firm. I badly want to talk to him, but I know I can't. All I can do is brood. I try not to think about it.

I'm like a snake shedding its skin. There was the "before" me who'd never been beaten up, had a sweetheart named Joey, and was generally happy. There was the "after" me who'd been beaten unconscious, lost innocence and dignity, and lost Joey. Now there is me after the revenge. I have yet to discover how that person will turn out.

I never liked the idea of therapy, even after my mom insisted. But I'm filled with so much emotion and I don't know how it's going to manifest itself. Can I resurrect who I was before?

At least the revenge gave me something to look forward to. It sounds sick, but for a long time that was what I clung to for comfort. I expected the empty feeling in my stomach to go away. But it didn't and still hasn't. The revenge gave me something to focus on. The small degree of happiness it afforded me has faded. Now I am, in a sense, right back where I started except that my friend Nick is in jail, and I've lost Joey. I feel as if I avenged myself for all the wrong reasons. My vision was clouded.

I had promised myself I wouldn't lose Joey as a result of what happened. Some promise that turned out to be. Now I have to say goodbye to Nick as well. It is too much. I dragged those two people into my nightmare. Nick came willingly with extendo bats, but it is still my fault.

As much as I wanted to distance myself from the whole thing, it is still around me. I watch the news every night hoping to hear some details about our actions. But there is nothing. That disturbs me even more. Those kids probably had to reach out to their parents for help and moral support. They are victims like me. Before my revenge, I wanted them dead. Now that reality has set in, I want them to be well. I didn't read the warning signs.

Every night I watch the news, and it all seems to be about faraway places. Bombings, terrorist acts, threats, and politics. But what about the war at home? There is no mention of what Nick, Kevin, and I had done. Not on the Internet, not on the radio, not in the campus newspapers, and not on television. It is like it never happened. I wasn't looking for validation or fame, but I was looking for some sort of acknowledgement.

* * *

Life goes on, as it does with me.

For perhaps two weeks it is just the usual routine. I notice a slight disconnect between Kevin and me, but it isn't enough to bring up. I have become more conscious of the relationships around me. I have lost Nick and Joey, but there is no way Kevin and I will drift apart.

One night in the kitchen after watching *Jeopardy,* I don't need to speak up, because Kevin does.

"How are you?" he says.

"Good. School is busy."

"Don't give me that, like you don't know what I'm really talking about."

Talk about going right for the jugular. He's serious. "It's tough, man," is all I can think to say. "I have this image in my head of us getting a medal or being knighted for what we did to those guys."

"It felt like you were teaching them a lesson," Kevin says.

"Yeah, but the more I think about it, it all meant nothing."

"It meant something to you."

"Who am I, a vigilante?"

"But you got what you wanted."

"It was what I wanted. I just wish I could take the whole thing back, everything, restart the year."

"That's the problem with life. There's no time machine."

Now I'm getting upset. "What does that mean? You didn't even help. All you did was watch."

"I came along, didn't I? You guys didn't need me for that."

"Then why did you come? I would've respected you more now if you hadn't."

"You want to know why I let you and Nick talk me into it? Because every time I thought of my best friend being beaten unconscious in the middle of the street, I got sick to my stomach. I wanted to see them get a dose of their own medicine. I wanted the sick feeling in my stomach to go away. But it didn't. It's still there."

He's not finished yet.

"I can't help but feel changed after what we did. I changed watching you beat those two guys without mercy. I had to pull you off them. You would've killed them. I changed that day. It showed me what animals we human beings really are. Most of all, I wanted my friend back. You know, it consumed you. I don't have to tell you that. You've let it take Joey and Nick from you."

"How do you know about Nick?"

"I got a phone call saying that punk kid Nick from high school finally got what he deserved."

"Is that how you really feel about him? Just some punk kid?"

"No, but who cares how I feel about Nick? The intentions, the feelings don't matter. It's what happened. And what happened is that Nick is now in jail."

I guess I'm not giving Kevin enough credit. He has a better grasp of things than I thought. But I'm not letting him off the hook.

"All right, then, if you have all the answers, what should I do now? Nick's going to jail, Joey has left, and I'm now arguing with what feels like my only friend in the world."

"We're not arguing. We're trying to make things right."

His words cut through everything.

"So make things right," he says. "Get your life back. Go get Joey back, and, when you get back to the city, visit Nick as often as you can."

Kevin's right. Things don't have to be so dramatic. There are still some wrongs I have to right, but they are honorable ones. Joey saw the dark cloud around me and wanted no part of it. Unfortunately I let it suck Nick and Kevin in. It was all a state of mind. But I have to work to be free of it. Shrugging off the past is impossible. I have to shake it off. I *need* to shake it off.

* * *

After talking to Kevin in the kitchen, I make a commitment to myself that I should have made a long time ago. I'm going to do the things I want to do. I'm not going to let society or anyone else influence me. I had let myself become a victim of culture, but now I have to break free.

This violence in me was not inborn: It was conditioned and then developed by me. I thought it was instinctive and natural to think like that. But the world isn't kill or be killed any more. At least not the world I want to live in. The only thing I was fighting for was peace of mind. I had a scarcity of peace. I was a victim of my culture, but I had only myself to blame.

The more justice I sought, the more hurt I became — because there is really no such thing as justice. It's make-believe. In society, if your country gets bombed, you retaliate. It just seems natural. But violence and revenge — they're not a straight line; they're a circle. There will always be a reaction. Even if you cut three heads off the serpent, one of them is bound to grow back.

I tried to cover all the bases, and in many ways I have. There's little opportunity for any of the events to come back to hurt me. Except for the effect on my mind. It's taken hold of one of the corners of my brain. I have to clear that part out. I have to excise it like Jim Carrey in *Eternal Sunshine of the Spotless Mind*.

There are steps I need to take, and they won't be easy. I'll have to swallow my pride. But it's easiest to move up when you start at the bottom. I have to rebuild. How do you manage decency? How do you maintain a moral code of behavior that you can fully embrace? The laws of society had failed me on two occasions. I don't need to find religion, but I do have to find my own truth, and I'm not going to find it just by talking about it in my kitchen with Kevin.

A certain calmness washes over me. These morals didn't need to be written down, they were physically beaten into me. As Carl Sandburg wrote, "I have seen the gunman kill and go free to kill again." Like him, I'll never again be "laughing even as an ignorant fighter laughs who has never lost a battle." The world is a serious place and not for the faint of heart.

Kevin had given me all the advice I needed. I had achieved

my moment of clarity. But my work has just started. I need to take action. I can't go back to my old world because my world has changed. I need to be responsive; I need to adapt, improve, make things better. If Joey cares for me the way I think she does, she'll still be carrying some demons. It's my duty to exorcise those for her. She had taken care of me; it's my turn to take care of her. There's little doubt she still carries the events of that night. She didn't know how to deal with me anymore. So she distanced herself. She got as far away from the dark cloud as she could.

She tried to help, and in many ways she saved my life. There's no good way to deal with a traumatic experience. But we have to find a way that works for both of us. I owe it to her to at least try to help.

At first I rationalize that the revenge was mostly for her, even though it was the last thing she wanted. She understood the whole situation best. She couldn't get me to understand. I was so stubborn. Maybe my guilt is overwhelming me now, but it's a feeling I can't ignore. Maybe I'm looking for something to take my attention off what happened to me and what I did to them. I guess when I tasted my desired victory, it turned out to be not as sweet as I had imagined.

I no longer understand why people enjoy hurting other people. That guy who goes to the bar wearing a shirt he doesn't care about, knowing in his heart that he's looking for an unfair fight to win, or that contract killer who murders a person he doesn't even know — how do they have the stomach for it?

I had become a victim of a culture that teaches violence is cool and that fighting is macho and the best answer to any problem. I needed to be more like the gang members in *The Warriors.*

They knew when they had to run and when they had to fight. That's what made the movie so great. The tension. They had to pick their moments. If they had fought every gang in the city, they wouldn't have stood a chance. They outsmarted their attackers. They used their wits first and fought only when they had to.

Now, I'm not some gang member from Coney Island. I'm a citizen, a student. This is what made everything so difficult to grasp. This sort of violence is generally not present in my life. So when it appeared, I had no way of dealing with it. It became the elephant in the room. I knew it was there, but I didn't know how to address it.

I'm getting off track. I'm losing sight of my first goal, of what's most important right now. I need to embrace the now. I need to focus.

Joey. I have no idea how she'll react to seeing me. It's been too long. What was I thinking when I let her go like that? Her leaving was the biggest warning sign of all. We haven't seen or talked to each other in what feels like forever. She may not even want to see or speak to me, but I'm prepared for that. Even if I use half the effort and motivation I used in my pursuit of a violent mistake, she'll have to acknowledge me. I'm not expecting her to leap back into my arms. That's unrealistic. I just want to tell her what she meant and still means to me. I want her to know that she was right. I want to hug her and thank her. I'm not going to lose another bond because of what I did. I have to go see my girl . . .

JOEY

13 I want to be prepared. I want to make sure I'm not lost for words when I see her. I have to make sure I say all the right things. If I have one hole in my attempt to thank her, the whole thing will be ruined. It has to be perfect. My previous attempts at perfection in situations dictated by emotion have failed. So, for this one, I'm shooting from the hip.

I decide to write her a letter. I don't know where I got the idea, but it embedded itself in my mind. The idea itself doesn't feel that cheesy. But actually sitting down and writing that letter about how I felt has the consistency of movie theater nachos.

I think about it for hours. Is this the best approach? Who writes letters anymore? And that is just it. Nobody writes letters anymore. In a world with email, voicemail, instant messaging, and Skype, nobody takes the time to send a nice handwritten letter.

Letters have a certain layer of romance surrounding them. That's why people always remember hate mail. It's true. You think, "Oh, how nice. Someone wrote me a letter," and then *boom.*

What can I write? There's no way I can sum up all the things that have gone on. I don't have writer's block. Quite the opposite: I have too much to say. I start thinking that often the best way to get a point across to someone is to tell a story. I'm going to write Joey a short story, but I have to phrase the letter in such a way that she can find her own meaning. It has to be like a Rorschach test. I know she loves the beach, so I run with that.

Dear Joey,
As I walk the beach, I stare out into the surf. The endless horizon. Things are good, I am calm. At peace. The water touches just the underside of my feet as my footprints are washed away in the sand. The waves crash with their own tempo and force. They're unpredictable but have a common pattern.

I look down the beach. I see a figure in the distance. I am drawn to it. It's the figure of a beautiful girl. I cannot look away. I need her, and I feel she needs me. My quick walk turns into a run. The gap is closing. We're almost together.

Who is she, and what's she doing here? All I know is that I need her. I can stay on this beach forever, as long as I'm with her. We're running toward each other, only twenty feet apart. We both slow our pace, gazing into each other's eyes. We walk the rest of the way right into each other's arms. We embrace and then share a perfect kiss.

She looks at me and smiles. She's happy. I'm happy. Our happiness can last only if we're together. I've found my paradise. I now know it isn't a place on any map. It isn't the beach or the surf or the sun setting on the horizon. It's how I feel for this moment with her. I want it to last forever.

Her smile fades. Something isn't right. She looks, but she can't see me anymore. In her eyes, I'm gone. She turns and runs away. I try to chase her. I try to bring her back to be with me, but I can't. She disappears over the horizon. She's gone.

I'm left empty. I'm alone on the beach. I've tasted paradise. I've felt true happiness. It was all with her. I walk on the beach. I stare out into the surf. The endless horizon. Forever searching for her. Forever trying to find just another moment with her, in paradise. She may never know that she saved my life.

Sappy, maybe. A good effort, certainly. Will it get her to at least call me? Definitely. It will remind her I still have a soul. That I haven't let this episode in my life destroy me. Maybe I need some reminding myself.

I fold the letter up neatly and place it in an envelope. Just writing her name on the envelope feels right. I'll hand deliver it, not to her personally, but to her door. I need to refresh her good memories of me before I start trying to make new ones.

Something occurs to me that brings my whole process to a standstill. What if she's already seeing someone else? That will make this letter incredibly awkward. But what's the worst thing that could happen? She won't speak to me, which is pretty much what is going on right now.

I have to do this. I have to at least try. I'll deliver it tomorrow afternoon. Joey has seen me at my absolute worst. I want her to remember what I was like at my absolute best, with her.

When you have free time and only one commitment for your day, all you can do is focus on that task. All day it sits there.

That one thing. Circled in your day planner, the only thing on the page.

The best thing to do is get it out of the way as early as possible. I want to deliver it as quickly as I can. Just like calling someone hoping for their voicemail, I'm going to deliver my letter to Joey and hope she isn't home.

I have a small breakfast and leave the house. I still have the morning layer of fuzz on my brain, which helps quiet my worries about possibly seeing her. My body is in motion, even though my mind is not firing just yet. But at the same time, I want to be sharp in case I do see her. I walk quickly, letter in hand. I am ready to start the first day of the rest of my life. I am at rock bottom and this is my first step on the path of righteousness. I feel free. I feel completely good for the first time in a long while.

The weather is overcast, but I respect Mother Nature's neutral feelings. It could get sunny or it could rain. For me, at least I'm trying to get a little light in my life instead of sitting in the rain. I'm doing something.

My good feelings multiply as I see friends on their daily journeys to class or to take care of errands. I am waving to people, shaking hands, exchanging pleasantries. All these encounters make me feel even better, as if I have a purpose. Here I am, back in the stream. I like it.

These interactions also help me forget about the walk and the task at hand. I'm getting close to Joey's now. Too close. It's not out of the realm of possibility that I'll run into her. My mind is so busy, I can barely concentrate on walking. Left foot. Right foot. I'm on her block. I'm in front of her door. My heart is pounding. I see the mailbox. I walk up her steps. Her door opens. Her door opens? Oh shit. Mayday. Mayday. It's Joey.

"Joey," I say.

I can see that she is startled. She grabs her chest in dramatic fashion. "What are you doing here?" she says.

Don't stumble. Be deliberate. Say what you need to say. "I came here to give you this." I extend the letter. "Please take it, Joey."

She hesitates. "What is it?"

Seems like a logical question.

"It's for you, please take it. I have to go."

She takes the letter. Yes! Transaction complete. I am in grade four handing out valentines to my favorite girls all over again. I'm giddy. I make a quick exit. She doesn't say anything else. I want to run, but I walk. My one worry, my one event for the day, is complete. Things are good. I have accomplished something. The first step on the road to recovery may have taken a while, but I've finally taken it.

Returning home, I want to skip like Mary Poppins. Life is about the small victories. I don't want to say that nothing can ruin the beauty of this day, so I don't. As I get back to my room, I want to sleep. I'm not tired. I'm full of excitement, and it's early in the day. But I want to go to sleep right now so nothing can happen that might tarnish things. Step one, day one has gone to plan.

I feel my phone vibrating in my pocket. Could this be Joey already? The display reads HOME CALLING.

"Hey, sweetie, how are you?" Mom says.

"Good. I'm having a good day. What's up?"

"Well, I don't want to be a downer on your day."

This usually means that the news will be a downer on my day. I read the tone of her voice. Her news isn't bad; it's just troubling. I can handle troubling.

"What is it, Mom?"

"It's Nick's dad."

I hope he's dead.

"He hasn't even tried to help out Nick's situation. No bail. No lawyer. No visits. Nothing. I'm not even sure he knows his son is in jail. He's just leaving him in there to fend for himself. All alone."

I'm not surprised.

"I want you to know we've done everything we can for him. Your father's even tried contacting Nick's dad, but because Nick is an adult, there really isn't much we can do."

I'm angry. A familiar feeling boils up inside. No. I can't let this put a blemish on the success of day one.

"I'm sorry, sweetie. I don't mean to ruin your day. I just thought you should know."

"You didn't ruin my day, Mom." Well maybe a little. "I'll be home soon to visit him. Please keep me posted on what's going on."

Mom can tell I don't really want to talk anymore. She tries to change the subject. Small talk. The weather. She wants me to forget what she just told me. But we both know I won't be forgetting it anytime soon.

After talking for five minutes with little input from me, she starts to wind down. I hear a beep on the line. It could be an opportunity to glide out of the conversation.

"Mom, I think you have a call coming in on the other line."

She checks. "No, must be you."

I pull the phone away from my ear and check the display. It reads JOEY CALLING.

I almost drop the phone. I can't believe she's called right away. I'm unprepared. I'm off guard. No script, I'll just be off the cuff, or shooting from the hip, or better yet, closer to the heart.

"Mom, I have to go, but I love you," I say, not waiting for a response.

I try to sound confused when I pick up the other call, as if I'm not sure who it is.

"Hi, it's me," Joey says.

It's me. Wow, we're back to that. I don't say anything. Control your enthusiasm.

"I read your letter. It certainly was a surprise, but thank you for writing it."

Yes!

"It said a lot and meant a lot. It made me miss you."

Hell, yes! I can't contain myself any longer. "Joey, that is so nice to hear. I've obviously missed you, too. Can I see you sometime soon?"

"How about we go for coffee sometime this weekend?"

This is perfect. "I'd like that a lot."

"Great, I'll give you a call Saturday."

Suddenly a light bulb goes off. "I can't do Saturday," I say. "I mean, I'm not here this weekend."

"Oh, OK then; some other time."

She's always so reasonable.

"Sorry, I just have to go home for something."

"Well, have a good weekend, and call me when you get back."

Her tone says whatever I am doing instead better be good.

I know that, Joey, I know that.

I'm not worried about pushing back seeing her. I have something else to do. Other plans. A favor to return. Something in my subconscious had hit me. A flash. My mind took over and ran on autopilot.

I remember walking to Nick's house one day after school when we were younger. I call it a house because, as I mentioned before, to call it a home would be a lie. His dad was there. I entered the house cautiously behind Nick, not wanting to step on any toes or upset the delicate balance of sanity in the house. It was like sneaking in past curfew, although it was broad daylight and there was no curfew. It wasn't love and warmth I was filled with as I entered the house, it was fear, and I didn't even live there. I couldn't even imagine coming home to that every day. It was like going to sleep every night knowing that you were going to have a nightmare.

As Nick walked past his excuse for a father, who luckily was asleep on the couch, he was careful not to kick any of the empty bottles on the floor. The living room was like a commercial for Alcoholics Anonymous. "Is alcohol ruining your family life?" Uh, yes.

Not being as sure-footed in Nick's house, I accidentally knocked one empty beer bottle into another, which made that unmistakable clinking noise. Of course Nick's dad woke up. It was probably the only thing that would wake him up. I remember his exact words to this day, and it was those words that flashed into my subconscious when I was talking to Joey.

Nick's dad looked Nick dead in the eye and said, "What do you want?"

Not "How was your day?" Not "How was school?" Just "What do you want?"

I was so mad at myself for waking him up.

All Nick said was, "Nothing."

I know that he wanted to say, "What I want is a dad who cares." But he didn't, and we got out of there as quickly as we could, not really remembering why we went there in the first place.

Nick didn't *want* a dad; he *needed* a dad. I owed Nick a lot. I had a debt to pay. I saw the good in him. I saw him for what he was: abused. For the longest time, I couldn't understand why his dad or anyone else wouldn't help him. No teacher or guidance counselor would help because their fear of him clouded their vision. Now he was in jail, right where everyone expected he would end up.

I know what I have to do. Step one on my road to true recovery is getting Joey back. If the authorities won't let me get Nick back, then I have to do the next best thing for my conscience. I have to confront Nick's dad.

It may sound stupid — another futile attempt to make things right, another effort with selfish undertones that will just make things worse. But I've done a lot of growing up. I've hit rock bottom. I'm not afraid of Nick's dad anymore. He's no longer a tremendous scary villain tormenting his own son. He's a pathetic, sad, bad excuse for a father who needs to look in the mirror.

I don't see myself as *The Punisher* or some superhero. I don't think I need to right all the wrongs in the world. You might see similarities to this and my previous desire for revenge. But this is different. I'll make it different. I'm going to make a change for good using good. And I'm not going to beat my head against the wall if it doesn't work. I'm going to move on.

I look at the wall in my bedroom which still has "Don't Stay Noble" taped to it. I remember waking up in the hospital and the old man. I tear the page off the wall. Crumpling it up feels good. I crush it in my hand before throwing it in the garbage. I even think about burning it.

The old man in the hospital had been right all along. His water bottle foreshadowed an inevitable turning point in my life. On a new piece of paper, I write, "Keep Calm and Carry On." All things considered, it seems like the best course of action. In a world full of sadness and tragedy, it seems that's all we can do.

Step two, confronting Nick's dad, is not going to be easy. The likelihood of success is probably low, but I have to try. In a strange way, I like my odds. I've faced evil within myself. I know what it looks like. I know how to channel it. The darkness that surfaced in my soul for a brief period was a reaction to somewhere I'd never been before. It was foreign, an unfamiliar feeling, but now I am no longer . . .

DEFENSELESS

14 This may sound odd to admit, but it's true. I'm afraid of getting hurt. I'm not like the tough, stoical cowboys of the cinema. Maybe I thought I was once.

Films victimized my mind. They showed me what I thought was appropriate behavior, but their world just isn't reality. In reality, the tough guy is the guy who helps out other people. The tough guy is the guy who tries to be a good father. The target of my thoughts right now is not a tough guy and definitely not a good father. He's a coward. For whatever reason, his grasp on reality has been skewed.

I understand that changing someone's mind is one of the most difficult things to do in the world. Especially when they've been set in their ways for a long time. But I have to try, for me and for Nick.

I have an image in my mind of how I want my interaction with Nick's dad to go, but I know I have to be ready for anything. A flying bottle, fist, or cigarette butt. To him I'm just a pest, a fly to be swatted. But I won't give up. I'll stay until I've said what I want to say. I'll do my best to make him understand.

I'm nervous, but I think being nervous is what keeps you alert and alive. On my bus ride home, I have a lot of time to think about the situation I would be walking into.

I have to do this. I haven't told my parents what I'm going to do, even though I really want to. I told them I need a break from school, so they aren't surprised to see me. Now I am walking on Nick's block with the same apprehension and sense of purpose I had when I was walking to Joey's.

Will he be home? I know exactly where he'll be: on the couch where I left him that day with Nick so many years ago. I'm determined. I'm focused. I'm standing in front of Nick's door about to knock. Here I am. Exactly where I need to be. It feels right. Whatever happens, I will "Keep Calm and Carry On."

I knock on the door three times, loudly. I'm not fooling around. Now are those awkward few moments. I hear rustling from behind the door.

"Who is it?"

He's home. I don't answer. Assuming he even remembers my name, I don't want him to know it's me. I hear him stumble over to the door. The knob turns. The door opens, and there he is.

He stinks of alcohol. His gut has doubled in size. He looks even more pathetic than I remember him being when I was in high school. What was I so afraid of back then?

"What do you want?"

If I was a Girl Guide selling cookies, would he have answered the door in the same manner? Probably.

I'm so filled with rage hearing that same phrase, I almost tackle him. But I don't want to miss my cue. Let's start the show.

"Mr. O'Gallagher, may I come in? It's about your son Nick."

"What's he done this time?"

"It's not what he's done. It's what you've done."

He is teetering. I have to keep him on balance before I really open up on him.

"And what's that?"

"Well, Mr. O'Gallagher, this will only take a minute. There was a young couple who just had their first baby, a boy. They'd bought a nice house with a pool in the backyard. They knew having a baby around a pool was dangerous, so they took every precaution. The boy . . ."

He's losing interest. I raise my voice. "The boy grew, Mr. O'Gallagher, and learned to walk. One day when the parents had their backs turned for only a few seconds, the boy got through the child-proof gate and into the pool. The boy drowned, Mr. O'Gallagher. There was nothing the parents could do. It wasn't their fault. They were devastated."

He interrupts me at the perfect moment. "What does that have to do with me or my son?"

Time to drop the hammer. "Unlike those parents, Mr. O'Gallagher, you've *let* your son drown. You filled his heart with so much fear that he sank. You're the reason he's in jail right now. All he wanted was for you to care, just a bit."

Nick's dad tries to shut the door. I stop him. He's retreating into the house.

"Help yourself and help your son. Save him before it's too late. Those parents never got the chance, Mr. O'Gallagher. You have a chance to do what's right. You have a chance to show him you care for once! How could you hit him? He was your baby boy!"

I let the door slam. It feels like the period at the end of a sentence. Complete.

That story about the young couple is true. I knew it would confuse or alert him enough to get his brief attention, or at very least, ruin his buzz. The young couple barely recovered from their loss. It almost tore them apart. But life goes on. From what my parents tell me, they're expecting their third child. Life goes on. Sad, tragic, terrible things happen every day — just watch the news. It's how we deal with them that counts.

Some things people never get over. Some things stay with them forever, but will fade with time. We're not invincible. The sad fact of life is that, if nothing bad has ever happened to you, you're defenseless until something does.

* * *

Sitting across from Joey, back at school having coffee, things could not be better. My demons have been exorcised, and I'm smiling. She's smiling. We're getting back to where we were. She knows something in me has changed and continues to comment on it. I agree with her. Life runs its course in a circle, and it all depends how each revolution starts. When you've gone back to the start, will you do better the second time around? Try to.

Joey and I leave, after talking for longer than either of us expected. As we're walking down the sidewalk, I feel her take my hand. Holding hands is not something I really enjoy doing; she knows that, but for right now it's perfect. I'm not the biggest fan of dancing either, but sometimes you just have to do it.

I recognize two faces coming toward us. I've seen them before. Their features alert my subconscious. I should have known. I should have spotted them a mile away. It's them: Departed One and Departed Two.

It's weird to even refer to them like that anymore. The funny way of the world continues to astound me. They're not out for revenge. They're out for a walk. They recognize me, and I recognize them. I'm not afraid. My heart rate does not even jump. They know the game was a loss. There were no winners. We cross paths and they continue on. No nod. No acknowledgement. I don't look back, and I know they don't either. I didn't hide my face. I'm free once again. I feel more calm than relief.

Joey didn't even notice, and I don't mention it. Why bother? "It's in the past," as my favorite character from *The Lion King* would say. I look at myself in a store-front glass display. I see us holding hands. I'm getting comfortable with this new guy holding Joey's hand. I've never met him before, but we're getting to know each other. I like his chances. All he has to do is keep taking steps in the right direction.

Two weeks after my little interaction with his father, I visit Nick. I don't tell him what I've done, but I think he knows somehow. He's happy to see me. I hate to hear him say it, but he kind of likes jail. All this scares me, but as long as we're still friends when he gets out, then I guess I'm OK. Nick won't be in there for long, I just know it. But he'll no doubt be different when he gets out. I try not to show my emotions.

"Thank your parents — they've been really good to me," he says.

"They only help because they know you have a good heart. You know, you don't have to be Mr. Blonde from *Reservoir Dogs*."

He laughs, knowing exactly what I'm talking about. "No, I'm worse."

"Just keep your head down in there, and you'll be out in no time." This is such a cliché. "Look at it this way, by the time you're out, I'll be done school and we'll both be back in the neighborhood. What a scary thought."

"You sure you're going to want to hang out with that convicted criminal, Nick O'Gallagher?"

"I'm sure I'll want to hang out with one of my best friends, Nick O'Gallagher."

He smiles. "This is your one and only visit, OK?"

"Nick, if you think I'm not going to visit you . . ."

He breaks in. "Remember that time we climbed on top of the high school for a smoke?"

"Yeah."

"Remember the view?"

"Yeah."

"Whenever you think of me, think of that, OK?"

"I'll be on top of the high school waiting."

This is a good time to make my exit; his spirits are high and so are mine.

"Don't get too used to things in here," I say as I turn to leave.

"I hope I don't — otherwise the first thing I'll do when I get out is poison one of my old man's drinks."

I throw the alley-oop and he slam dunks it. His comment is

about as serious as it could be. He means it with every ounce of his being, but in a way he knows he would never do it.

"You are so much better than he is. And he knows that. Don't think about him. He deserves to be in jail more than you."

"That beating you took, I've been taking those my entire life."

"And I promise, on our loyalty, you'll never have to take a beating from him again."

Leaving the jail, I feel like going over to Nick's dad's house and killing him. I imagine it vividly. I'd use a shotgun (although I don't have one) and shoot him right in the chest. It would accomplish two things: one, Nick would no longer have him in his life, and two, I'd get to see Nick every day in jail. I figure Nick has had this thought more than a few times. But that was something out of a movie, not real life.

I tried to protect my friend when we were growing up the way he'd protected me. Only now I was certain I could. I mean that promise. It is something I had to get off my chest. I will make sure Nick's dad would no longer be a factor in his life. We'll both be free from the demons that had haunted us. Nick's pain had lasted most of his life. I was making sure mine wouldn't haunt me for another day.

* * *

When I look back now at what happened, it all seems to be for a reason. I don't really buy into cosmic philosophies or religious theories, but it must be said that the world works in mysterious ways. In a perfect world, we'd only be in hospital once, at birth.

I feel like the place I'm in right now is the right place, the perfect place for me. I didn't know how to deal with the cards I was dealt. I think and believe that great people are defined by their ability to turn a bad outcome into a good one. I want to be great. The world is full of bad stuff, and it can be overwhelming. To survive, we all have to be spin artists, spinning a positive thread of whatever fabric the world gives us while we're here. Every day we're plunged into the fire. All we can do is look for comfort.

I'll take care of my loved ones. I'll live with integrity and take the right steps in the right direction. My ideal will be real. I want to go home. I'm home now. I'm finally going to have my *simple kind of life.*

AUTHOR'S NOTE

Like the narrator, I was the victim of a violent attack when I was twenty-one. All of the other details about the narrator are fictional. I wrote this book for any victim who never got the answers or results they deserved. A coward's motives are irrational to you because you have honor. Your compassion is something your attackers do not share. That's why it is so important. It separates you from them.

I recovered and learned that revenge is just a small circle and life goes on.

CPSIA information can be obtained at www.ICGtesting.com
Printed in the USA
LVOW132130310812

296904LV00006B/21/P

9 781927 483121